Beguile Me Not

ODELIA FLORIS

Also by Odelia Floris

Adult fiction:
The Heart of Darkness
(The Chaucy Shire Medieval Mysteries, Book 1)

Children's fiction:
The Little Demon Who Couldn't

Nonfiction:
Inspiration & Wisdom from the Pen of Ralph Waldo Emerson:
Over 600 Quotes

www.odeliafloris.com

Copyright ©Odelia Floris 2014
SECOND EDITION

All rights reserved. No part of this book may be copied, reproduced, stored in a retrieval system, or transmitted in any form or by any means, without the prior written consent of the author.

# 1

At That Fateful Hour

ANNA lifted the crinkled leaf of paper up to her nose and drew a slow, deep breath. The familiar mingled scent of cologne, paper and cigar smoke wrapped her in longing, in pleasure, and in a sadness that was somehow happiness at the same time. She then carefully unfolded the small cream note.

Moving across to the open window in order to allow the last of the evening light to fall upon it, she passed her eyes over the free, decisive script. Her lips moved silently as she read the words, which were now etched in her mind. Then she closed her eyes and leaned back against the window frame as vivid memories of that summer night at the ball and the days that followed it engulfed her, and in memory she was back there once more.

'I really am rather disappointed with the quality of the young gentlemen here this evening,' her mother had been saying as she leaned close in close to her friend and fellow son-in-law hunter, Mrs Bingham. 'One would think that a grand ball like this would have had a much better showing.'

'Yes, quite,' Mrs Bingham replied in hushed tones, anxious not to be overheard.

Anna's mother suddenly turned to her daughter with the look of a cat that has just sighted a mouse. 'My dear,' she cried, seizing Anna by the elbow, 'what about him?'

Anna frowned across at the ballroom's crowded entranceway. 'Who?'

'That young man with the brown cravat who has just entered. I hear he has quite respectable means!'

'But Mother, he looks as old as Uncle William!'

Mother gave her shawl a huffy, annoyed hoick. 'It is clear that the gentleman is a little older than you are, but he is still a respectable match. It is not as if you have had any better offers recently!'

Anna opened her fan and wafted it wretchedly. Mother's all-too-frequent frustrations were starting to make her head ache already. 'It is not my fault if there is a lack of eligible young men in this dreadful little colony.'

'There are eligible young men; it is simply that you will not accept them. That nice bank manager, Mr Lawson, who proposed to you last year—you should have accepted!'

The evening had barely begun but already Anna wanted to go home. She sighed wearily. 'But Mr Lawson was such a bore. The only things he ever talked about were his bank and his wretched dead butterfly collection.'

'It is all well and good for you to scoff at poor Mr Lawson, my dear, but marrying him would be better than ending up an old maid!' Mother wailed, her air of hurt indignation heightening.

Anna put a soothing hand on her mother's arm, hoping the handkerchief she held was not about to be dispatched on duty. 'Do not trouble yourself about me, Mother dear. I am only twenty-seven. I am sure I shall find a suitable match before long.'

But Mother was in no mood for being comforted. 'Only twenty-seven! Really, my dear, what are you waiting for? A prince? Is that the only kind of man whom you think is good enough for you?'

Anna's head positively pounded. 'No! You know I am more practical than that.'

With her chin still tilted up in the manner of one determined not to be appeased, Mother turned away. 'I really must sit down. All this effort trying to find a husband for my thankless daughter has *quite* worn me out already.'

'Oh Mother...' Anna whined after the matron's receding back.

But Mother took no notice.

Anna stepped up her fanning in an effort to ease her throbbing head.

She felt such a wretch. All of her sisters, even the younger ones, had already made excellent matches, yet she still languished on the shelf. And, without wishing to dishonour her, Mother really was being harsh. It was not so much a general lack of bachelors that was the cause of the difficulty, but the Brown family's high standards. There is nothing more likely to dampen the ardour of a suitor than the feeling that both the girl and the girl's mother regard the size of his purse with scorn and think his pedigree more mongrel than thoroughbred.

Slowing her fanning to a soothing rhythm, Anna swept regally down the near-empty side gallery. She could not help admiring her fine violet silk gown and slim waist as she passed a large, gilded mirror.

Mother was quite right to wish nothing but the best for her daughters, Anna reassured herself. After all, the Browns were one of the wealthiest and most respectable families in Auckland. When you have been brought up in the largest house in a neighbourhood of large houses, you are accustomed to a certain civilised standard of living. As Mother was always saying, a husband who cannot keep his wife in the manner to which she is accustomed is sure to result in an unhappy home.

Anna was soon interrupted from the task of admiring her extravagantly arranged dark brown hair by another young lady sailing into the gallery.

'Miss Anna, how delightful to see you!' cried the red-gowned blond.

The weak smile Anna turned on the new arrival almost suggested her presence was unwelcome. 'How do you do, Miss Dora.'

'So, have you spotted any worthy fish to cast your line at?' asked the smiling, rosy-cheeked Miss Dora Bingham.

Anna's limp fanning resumed. 'No, although Mother was terribly keen to throw me at some man old enough to be my father.'

'Oh dear,' the blonde girl replied brightly. 'I really am expecting to pick up the newspaper one morning and have my eyes alight on an advertisement reading, "wanted: man. Must be very much alive and in possession of a good fortune. Please send replies to Mrs Winston Brown, Elton Towers, Auckland." '

The fanning grew stronger and jerkier. 'Mother merely wants the best for me.'

'Mother *merely* wants society to coo over the good match she has made for her daughter, and have grandchildren with good bloodlines,' said Miss Dora, raising her eyebrows archly.

Anna abruptly flicked her fan shut and eyed Miss Dora hostilely. 'It does not surprise me that you, Miss Dora, have yet to find a husband. No man would wish to marry a young lady who always thinks the worst of people. No husband wishes to be criticised every waking hour.'

To Anna's great surprise, Miss Dora simply laughed. 'I do not care for husbands and would quite happily be an old maid. I could start a home for orphans or some such lark!'

Anna had always thought Miss Dora slightly unhinged. She was a wild romantic. Mooning around reading novels and poetry all day was bad for one. It bred subversive, impractical ideas. But one must never be impolite, and this conversation was overstepping polite boundaries. If it carried on like this, someone might even have an original thought.

She forced her drooping lips into a smile. 'Have you got any names on your dance card yet, Miss Dora?'

'Oh yes! Let me see…' The blithe blond consulted the pink card dangling from her wrist. 'There is Teddy for the Polka, Lawrie for the waltz, Mr Simons for the two-step, and Teddy again for the mazurka.'

Anna's own blank dance card gave her pride a painful poke. A quickly filled dance card was a true badge of honour for a young lady. She prayed none of her friends would enquire after her own dance card before the problem could be rectified. And to rectify it she needed to get amidst the glittering throng in the main ballroom and display herself.

'Miss Dora, you must excuse me. Delightful as conversing with you is, I really ought to mingle a little.'

Anna tiredly lifted her weighty skirts and began a slow passage towards the gallery exit, like a ship of the line under full sail.

An irritated sigh escaped her. The nine years since her début into society had been spent in an endless round of balls, dinner parties, soirées and social calls. Like a farmer with a prize heifer, Mother trotted her out on every possible occasion. At first, it had been a gay, exciting delight. But now a certain ennui had overtaken Anna. The same people, the same places, the same conversations…it had grown into a seemingly endless toil. The ennui worsened by the day.

After a lengthy stint of parading, smiling and seductive fanning, Anna only managed to gain two entries on her dance card. And not very pleasing entries at that.

With a cool drink in hand, she sunk onto a sofa in the corner to rest a little. Perhaps her mother and sisters were right. Perhaps she was too serious, too aloof. And while she was comely enough, her beauty was of a quiet kind, a somewhat ordinary kind.

The waltz was announced. She rose, ready to take the hand of her partner.

A balding gentleman of about fifty wearing a brown cravat hurried over. 'This dance, I believe, is mine?'

She gave an inclination of the head, which she was afraid failed to conceal some frostiness.

After an irritating waltz during which conversation was stilted and Anna's shoes gained some new scuffs, she was mercifully released. Feeling strangely tearful and with her head aching, she made for the open door leading out onto the veranda.

As she stepped out, the cool air of the midsummer night washed over her in a welcome wave that was a blessed relief after the hot, close air of the crowded ballroom, which seemed to cling about one and squeeze the life out of one's limbs.

She followed the veranda around to the front of the grand house. There, the mysterious sounds of the night mingled with the faint music and gay laughter drifting out from the ballroom.

The weary ball-goer leaned against the balustrade and gazed out over the moonlit garden below. The dull, empty ache she fought with increasing frequency filled her. Mother had told her what the cause of the ennui, of the vague longing, was. It was the lack of a husband. The lack of an establishment of her own. She needed to be married so she could busy herself organising dinner parties and pushing her husband up in the world by carefully cultivating the right social contacts. It was the lack of children, and of a man to keep a firm hand on her. A woman without a man, Mother told her, was like a ship without a captain, like a horse without a rider. Questioning your parents was wrong. Yet why did Mother's advice only seem to make the aching emptiness worse?

Wishing to be even more alone, she swept down the steps and out onto the paved terrace below. An arbour enclosed the terrace on three sides, while the fourth offered a view over the garden slopes below. The thick, exotic, milky-sweet fragrance of jasmine hung in the breathlessly still night air.

She leaned against the arbour, buried her nose in a spray of white jasmine flowers and revelled in the deliciously cloying perfume. But a moment later a sigh of wind rustled through the darkened garden, and carried on that breeze was the scent of cigar smoke.

Anna lifted her head abruptly and looked about. There, with his back turned to her, stood a man. He was in the process of extinguishing a cigar in an ashtray resting on the arbour's balustrade.

Anna frowned. Who was this unwelcome companion? Ah yes— she had briefly seen that smart dark burgundy jacket and thick silver hair among the guests as she began the waltz. Before the preservation of her toes demanded all her attention.

She sighed. How tiresome. Another elder statesman to bore her.

Loathe to be subjected to the patronising attentions of some patriarch, she quickly wiped the evidence of her tears away with careful gloved fingers.

But the gentleman who now faced her was too young to be either a boring elder statesman or a patronising patriarch.

He stepped out of the shadows and, with a hand still un-gloved from smoking, took her hand and bowed gracefully as he kissed it. '*Enchantée*, mademoiselle.'

His French was impeccable. Surely he was a native speaker?

Feeling stiff with surprise and uneasy about having been unwittingly observed, she gave a solemn nod. 'I am Miss Anna Brown.'

He clicked his heels together and gave another slow, graceful bow. 'Alexander Ivanovsky at your service, Miss Anna.'

While his English was excellent, it was clearly accented. The accent was not French. The voice was warm, rich and impossibly smooth, and the pronunciation heavy and ponderous, with hard consonants and soft vowels that melted through his words like thick honey. She had never heard someone speak like that before. Ivanovsky? Why, of course, he had to be Russian!

A little annoyed at her slowness, Anna frowned. She did not like to be puzzled. 'Delighted, Mr Ivanovsky.'

But Anna had lied. She was not delighted. Mr Ivanovsky disturbed her. She felt like an explorer who had suddenly found themselves face-to-face with a strange, never-before-seen creature.

Mr Ivanovsky had a thick head of silver hair, yet he looked less than forty. The shock he received must have been truly terrible to cause such a thing. Mr Ivanovsky was tall and broad-shouldered as an oak tree, with a powerfully muscled neck that would have been brutish on many men, but in him was mixed with a gentleness that made it merely strong.

He was also much too handsome. His features were smoothly full, considered in their strength, and his dark brows thoughtfully heavy, his lips sensitively full and perfectly formed.

And the eyes. The soulful dark brown eyes were peaceful and drowsily hooded, yet still seeming to miss nothing. There was something arrestingly otherworldly about that face, yet not in an ethereal way. This other world was the hidden kingdom of the deep-rooting fir tree, the otherworld of the life-giving soil that nourished the shimmering cornfield and the blossoming cherry.

Mr Ivanovsky smiled. The smile was warm, sad, secretively knowing and slightly reserved. A smile that could have melted ice. 'Why so melancholy?'

She almost gasped. So direct. So exposingly direct. 'I…I…am merely feeling a little hot. The air inside, so terribly close…'

'Pardon me for disturbing your mournful thoughts earlier. I was not lurking down here with sole intention of killing your moment of respite.'

Anna suddenly remembered Mrs Bingham mentioning a Russian who might be at the ball. A Russian guest who was an artist commissioned by a wealthy patron to paint the New Zealand landscape. And everyone knows that artists are always poor and of obscure origins. This man was a humble artist, not some marauding Slavic warrior come to carry her off. She was pleased to find her usual unsinkable social composure returning.

She gave a smile that she believed was gracious, although others might have thought it was frosty and rather patronising. 'Thank you, Mr Ivanovsky. I am feeling quite recovered now. I think I shall return to the ball before I am missed.'

He gave a gracious inclination of the head. 'You are welcome, mademoiselle.'

She turned to leave, but his quiet, reflective voice forced her to stop if she wished to remain polite.

'There is no need to be afraid of sadness, Miss Anna. Sadness holds many beautiful things for those with will to uncover them.'

She heard a nervous laugh escape her. What nonsense the man was talking! Sadness is good, indeed. Artists clearly were every bit as mad as respectable people said they were.

'Really, I was merely feeling a little faint from the heat!' she replied with a forced blitheness that attempted to conceal deep unease.

'When soul cries out in protest at the bonds encircling it, we must pause to listen.'

His manner was quiet and thoughtful, but much, much too intimate and familiar for her liking. Things she did not understand made Anna afraid, and she did not understand Mr Ivanovsky. He was somehow different to anyone else she had ever met. She did not know why, but he was.

Pulling her aloof manner more closely about her, Anna cleared her throat. 'Quite. Now, I really must get back to the ballroom.'

The Russian's ponderous mood seemed as though it was rooted in the very earth. His peaceful dignity remained unaffected by her frosty unease. 'Might I request the pleasure of next dance?'

It would break her unwritten rules, which stated that energy must not be wasted on gentlemen who are not eligible bachelors. But then again, there were ten dances to go and only one entry on her dance card. One did not want to risk appearing a wallflower. That would not do at all.

She sighed. 'Yes, you may have the slow waltz.'

He smiled his dangerous-to-ice smile. '*Merci.*' Then he offered his arm.

She cautiously slipped her gloved hand under his elbow.

'In Russia, we often call loved one bearing the name Anna "Anya",' he said, as he led her back up the steps. 'I think you look like you need a friend, so I shall call you Anya.'

She was speechless. They had only met a moment ago and already he was giving her a diminutive form of her name! People simply did not *do* that.

He glanced down at her with his drowsy, heavy-lidded eyes. 'You, Miss Anya, must call me Sasha. All of my friends do.'

Fortunately for Anna, she was spared from having to find a suitable response to this latest horror. They had entered the ballroom now, where the orchestra was just beginning the slow waltz.

She smiled the fixed smile she used on occasions when gaiety was expected, and held her hand out to her dance partner.

Ivanovsky soon had Anna in his arms and was whirling her around the dance floor. Her earlier unease at his informal manner melted away as he proved himself an excellent dancer. He was light on his feet, held himself with elegance, and guided her around the crowded floor with confidence. Most impressively of all, her shoes were untouched.

She was swept into the pulsing, swaying rhythms of the music as though caught up in an invisible river. The joy of the dance filled her as her feet flew across the floor, and once again she felt the pleasure dancing used to bring before an endless file of dull partners and bruised toes eroded it.

Dancing with Ivanovsky, she felt as though she was dancing with the music itself. The slow waltz ended and a fast polka began. Without even thinking, Anna started the new steps. He expertly joined her and led her through a fast twirl. She laughed aloud with joyous abandon.

He laughed his low, honeyed laugh and smiled tenderly down at her. 'Tonight, I think the music plays only for you.'

'I feel like a young girl again...' she breathed, leaning back and plunging even deeper into the driving, passionate rhythms.

'Little darling, you *are* young girl.'

Dance followed dance, and Anna danced every one of them with Ivanovsky, oblivious to anyone else in the room. She was enfolded in a world of joy that contained only her, Ivanovsky and the soaring, lilting music. All the while they danced, his eyes barely left hers for a moment as he told her of Russia, of his home in Saint Petersburg, of his travels in Australia and Tahiti, and of his planned travels in New Zealand.

When the music stopped at last, Ivanovsky led the flushed, breathless, laughing Anna out into the coolness of the night air on the veranda. He put his arms around her waist and smiled his meltingly fond smile down at her. 'My darling Anya, tonight has been like dream...'

Wrapped in the loving, thoughtful glow of his presence, she let his languid, richly thick voice, which seemed to caress the very words he spoke, wash over her. 'Oh Sasha, I never want this dream to end...'

'Anna, we are leaving now!' Mother's loud call reached out through the doors.

Anna's breath caught painfully in her throat. She did not want to go. But almost all the other guests had left. And her joy, her dream, had to leave too. 'Goodbye, Sasha. This evening was magical, I will always remember—'

'Anna, come here at once!'

'I will always remember my midsummer night's dream…'

Then she was gone.

* * * *

Resisting the urge to simply throw herself down on the park bench, Anna instead carefully closed her parasol, leaned it against the seat and sat down with genteel dignity. The walk across the park to the bench and back was taken every afternoon, weather permitting. This summer day was terribly hot, and the uphill walk had left Anna feeling breathless and very sticky. The shade of the tall elm tree overhead was most welcome.

She had been feeling rather breathless ever since the ball four days ago. Breathless with horror. Breathless with mortification at the flock of wagging tongues her behaviour had set in motion. She had even heard a distant rumour that Miss Anna Brown was on the verge of eloping with a penniless Russian émigré. They could at least get a few simple facts straight: Mr Ivanovsky was merely on a prolonged visit. Furthermore, Anna was filled with horror at the speed and ease with which she had forgotten even the most elementary rule of respectable society—that how things appear to others is of primary importance. What had happened to sensible Anna, practical Anna, respectable Anna? She had shamed herself and her family. Thinking of it made her skin crawl and a strange tightness close around her throat.

She sighed wretchedly and mopped her perspiring brow. That hot summer night at the ball, it seemed as though a spell had descended on her. She did not like it; she did not like it at all. Everything must be under strict control at all times. No emotion must escape.

'You must pardon me for disturbing you once more, Miss Anya.'

She snapped her head around. He was standing right behind her, cane and hat in hand. Anna almost yelped in fright. Almost. 'Mr Ivanovsky!'

Smiling the sad, loving smile that often hovered on his lips, he bowed politely. 'How terrible of me to startle you like this once again. I hope you can forgive me.'

Realising she had seized her parasol and was holding it like an Amazon about to storm a citadel, Anna let her breath out and placed the thing down. 'Mr Ivanovsky, I was...was...merely lost in thought.'

He indicated the space beside her. 'You do not mind if I sit?'

'Ahem, not at...all.'

She did mind. She minded a great deal. Being faced with the cause of her fall from the paragon of respectability pedestal was almost unbearable. The thought of all those people talking about her, talking about how shocking she was—it made her feel like she was choking.

'I believe I may have overlooked the viciousness of public opinion in this town and the ruthlessness of its gossips.'

The lump in her throat was so strong she could barely swallow.

'In d-deed.'

'You must not concern yourself with the opinions of others, Anya.' He uttered this quietly, with the mix of strength and softness so particular to him. 'This scandal is petty, mere chaff on the wind, and like child's tantrum, will soon be forgotten. One must not a live a life whose merit is judged by good opinions of others. Listen to your own conscience, not petty judgements of gossips.'

To Anna's horror, tears started to roll unstoppably down her hot cheeks. 'I can think of nothing else day and night except people *talking* about me, and what is worse is that I cannot bear it when people look at me! All I can think of is what they must be thinking!' Almost sobbing aloud, she leapt to her feet. 'This is intolerable—I feel as though I will die if one more word about the ball is spoken! We must never speak to one another or be seen together ever again! Do you understand?'

After a moment's silence, he nodded sadly. 'I will do as you wish. I will leave town at earliest possible moment.'

Feeling as though she was shrivelling up with humiliation, Anna desperately wiped at the tears streaming down her checks. But they just would not stop coming. 'Thank you,' she gasped, between stifled sobs.

'I hope you can believe that I had no part in any rumours which have spread about you. I have spoken of you to no one.'

Pressing a handkerchief to her face, she nodded miserably and sat back down.

He placed a kindly hand on her arm. 'You must not heed vindictive, narrowed-minded imaginings of others with nothing better to do than senselessly gossip. Anya, you are virtuous young woman. You must hold your head up regardless of what others say.'

Anna suddenly buried her face in her hands. 'Mother called me a wonton disgrace to the family name!'

'Oh Anya, I am so sorry to have been cause of this. But unless being happy is sin, you did nothing wrong at the ball.'

'I wish you were right—I hate you!' She turned away from him with a fierce jerk and buried her head in her arms as she positively howled.

'And I love you…' came his quiet, tender response.

Her crying paused abruptly as shock took its place. 'No, no—go away!' The howls resumed.

'As you wish. I will never approach you again, of that you have my word. Adieu, Anya. I hope that one day you find the peace you were searching for out in moonlit garden that night.'

After a safe interval, Anna finally looked up. Ivanovsky's tall figure was just about to disappear from view behind the trees at the far end of the cricket field.

She waited in silence until he vanished from view, then flung herself down and howled louder than ever.

* * * *

Sinking down onto the park bench, Anna stared across the cricket field to the trees at its far end. The previous afternoon's image of Ivanovsky's receding figure seemed to be burned into her mind. All through the hot, airless night it had been there. She had not slept a wink and she did not know why. She never wished to see

Ivanovsky ever again—at least that was what she had silently repeated to herself all through the lonely night hours.

Feeling completely wrecked, she lay down on the bench and stretched out. But something smooth, hard and rounded was beneath her hand. Frowning, she held the thing up. It was a Russian doll.

The frown deepened. Russian? Ivanovsky had left it there!

She stared grimly at the brightly painted doll's innocently smiling face. It made Russians seem so normal, so safe. Russians were neither normal nor safe. Russians should be avoided at all costs.

Why had he left it there? Ah yes...didn't Russian dolls have things inside them?

With shaking hands, Anna unscrewed the cheerful little doll. Inside was another, smaller, doll—and a note.

The note smelt of Ivanovsky. The scent threatened to drag her back to the ball. Back into Ivanovsky's arms. She clung desperately to the present and forced herself to start reading:

Darling Anya

As I write this, I am packing to leave on the steamboat tomorrow. I am sorry that my last sight of you was so sad. I hope that you have forgiven me.

Dearest one, you are stronger than you know. Do not be afraid of the shadowy depths of your soul. Treasures lay hidden in the deep as well as horrors, and the night conceals many beauteous things. My sweet one, you are much wiser than you know. Listen to the voice that calls to you from within, for there you will learn secrets no one else can tell you.

I hope that one day you will face the deep without fear and find a way to be at peace. I will cherish and love your memory always.

I kiss this for you and send it with a hundred more kisses and good wishes.

Always
your Sasha

Anna felt something melt within her. Trying to hate him was futile. It was simply not going to work. The man was an angel of kindness. She would just have to erase every thought and memory of him from her mind instead.

Then she looked at the unopened smaller doll. Surely he had not? With fingers almost rattling with fear, she unscrewed the smiling doe-eyed doll.

Inside was a note. It too smelled of Ivanovsky. Her eyes raced over the shaking note:

Ah, you little darling, you sweet one, why does your image burn in my mind? Why do your sad grey eyes haunt my dreams? A thousand stars fill the sky above, and I am filled with a thousand thoughts of you.

The breeze whispers in the birch tree and I am back at the ball, watching you stand listlessly sighing on the balcony. The cool leaves in the garden brush against my skin, and I feel your trembling touch once more.

As the moon burns on the horizon and the sleeping world is embraced by the night, my soul burns for your presence and memories of you press themselves close about my heart.

At last the rosy dawn comes to stir my sleepless languishing. Ah, you little darling, you sweet one, will you not give my soul the bliss it yearns for?

Anna stared at the note. The very paper it was written on seemed to breathe love.

Trying to forget him was futile. She would just have to carry on living. Carry on living in the way her family expected her to. Carry on living in the way polite society expected her to. Carry on living in the way she expected herself to.

She tucked the cologne-and-cigar scented notes into the bosom of her dress, put the Russian doll into her pocket, unfurled her parasol, rigidified her trembling lips, and marched forward.

* * * *

The light had now faded so much that Anna could no longer see the words on the note. With a sigh, she walked over to the writing desk. There, she pressed the note to her lips and breathed in Ivanovsky's familiar, comforting, although by now faint, aroma one last time.

The note was then tenderly folded, placed back into its wooden nest and the two halves of the smiling Russian doll reunited.

This routine was a very familiar one now. Anna had been doing it every night for the past six months. But not for much longer. When she was married, she would have other duties to perform before going to sleep. A wife could not be seen crying and sighing over a love letter from an old flame, especially if that past love happened to be the only man she had ever loved, the man she still burned a candle for deep in the most secret corner of her heart.

Two weeks from now all thoughts of feeble, doomed, faraway loves would have to be put away, just as a girl must put away her dolls upon reaching womanhood. That candle would have to be extinguished, and Mr Sleighman allowed the privileges a husband expected.

Anna shuddered distastefully and pulled the bedclothes tight up around her neck. After a lengthy period of tossing and turning, the distant pounding of the waves finally lulled her into a fitful sleep.

2

How Dismal

THE next day after luncheon, Anna readied herself for her afternoon walk by firmly tying her bonnet on. She had given up on parasols after the wind wrecked the third one. Parasols might have functioned in the park opposite Elton Towers, but Aramoana Beach was not so kind.

The wind snatched at her skirts as soon as she closed the front door of Gravemore House behind her. But she braced herself and defiantly walked into its face, crossing the lawn and passing through the small gate leading into the paddock beyond.

The short, tough grasses covering the paddock were already browning, even though it was only late November. At this rate, there was going to be a dreadful drought come summer. She had heard her brother-in-law just that morning. He had said the hills would bake to hard, cracked clay, and grass fires were a real possibility.

As if it was not bad enough here already. She wrinkled her nose at the sheep scattered about the paddock. She hated sheep. They were stupid, dirty, and worst of all was the smell. She hated the smell of sheep.

This was not conducive to her happiness. Gravemore was, after all, a sheep station. A very large sheep station with a very large number of sheep.

Thankfully the paddock was not large, and soon she was trudging through the tussock-dotted sand dunes. At least half a sand dune got down her shoes, but she had to wait until she had reached the wet sand before she could get the shoes and their furiously irritating extra guests off. The dry sand was simply much too hot to walk on barefoot.

Anna turned to look back the way she had come. Gravemore Station's large, two-storied homestead lay in the middle of the flat, brown-grassed paddock like a beached white whale. The trees and gardens which promised to someday surround it were still but a scattering of stalks, saplings and seedlings.

The steep hills soaring up behind Gravemore were even browner. Tombstone-like tree stumps lingered on here and there, and a scattering of tree trunks lay like the bleached bones of fallen warriors left unburied on the battlefield upon which they fell. These last remnants of the once-mighty forest that had marched from the seashore to the mountains inland filled Anna with a deep melancholy. The landslide-scarred pasture that had taken the place of the ancient forest seemed so meagre, so pitiful, so cruel.

Turning back towards the east soothed her offended eyes. The beach was one of the few things about Gravemore Station she did not actively dislike. The other thing Anna liked about Gravemore besides the sea was the fact that no one there knew about her night of shame at the ball or any of the gossip that it had bred. It really was marvellous.

Anna's relationship with the ocean had not been a case of love at first sight. She had arrived at Gravemore last June, when winter storms whipped the sea into a foaming frenzy and the sandy beach was pounded by large waves that raced each other in a mad dash to hurl themselves to their deaths on the shore.

These winter seas had made her afraid at first. They were too wild, too furious, too unfettered. But little by little the ocean had drawn her into its bewitching rhythms and moods. The bracing salty winds that often blew were so bright and clean that it was almost as if the air itself sparkled. The sound of the waves was a soothing music that spoke of primal creation and eternal rhythms. It was a siren song that drew her down to the seashore every day.

It had been the faintest of whispers at first, but now this siren song had grown into an entrancing call that pulled at the deepest part of her. It called to the vague longing that lay buried inside. It cajoled, it teased, it sighed. *Come, oh come to me*, the waves seemed to murmur. *Become at one with me. Fuse your soul with mine. Plunge into my mystery. Come, come and let me bear you far, far away. Far away to distant shores, far away to distant dreams which now are only faint echoes in your heart.*

But Odysseus was not the only one with a mast to lash himself to. The conventions of polite society and the expectations of her family provided Anna with a mast stout enough to rival the Greek hero's. Nothing was more dear to her than the good opinion of society.

With great self-satisfaction, Anna thought about how dutiful and obedient a daughter she was being. She had had no personal desire to visit her sister Jennifer and her husband at their remote sheep station on the North Island's East Coast. But after a four-month stay with her aunt in the town of Napier which had failed to result in even a single offer of marriage, Mother and Father had decided Anna was to be bundled off to Gravemore Station for a lengthy visit. A visit lengthy enough for any gossip about how Miss Anna Brown had gone quite wild to die away. A visit lengthy enough for her to get engaged to the Reverend Sleighman.

Mr Sleighman was the vicar of the little church at Aramoana Beach, and more importantly, his father was a bishop. Mr Sleighman was sure to become a bishop himself in time. Everyone said so. At present, Mr Sleighman was merely doing his saintly missionary duty of converting the natives in the wilderness before returning to Auckland in a blaze of glory to take his rightful position at God's right hand—or rather his father's, which seemed to be the same thing in the eyes of many.

After a long walk that took her all the way up to the north end of the beach and back, Anna took one last look at the ocean, pushed down the boisterous waves' beguiling whispers one last time, and turned back into the sand dunes.

She had better hurry. Mr Sleighman would be here for afternoon tea any minute. It was not proper to keep one's future husband waiting.

A hurried change out of her wrinkled sand-and-seawater covered muslin dress and into a large-bustled lavender one later, and Anna was seated in the front parlour.

She smoothed her gown, picked up a magazine, threw it back down, checked the clock. Ten minutes past four.

She sighed fitfully and rose. A few turns up and down the empty parlour, and then she paused before the mirror above the mantelpiece. Yes, that fair skin was still pale pink despite the harsh light out here. She turned her head to the side, tilted it up again, relaxed her rosebud lips into the moody, ponderous expression they looked so well in. That blush pink skin really was something to be proud of...

Suddenly, Anna realised the sounds of a visitor being shown in were coming from the hall.

A moment later and 'Mr Sleighman!' announced the maid.

The said man entered the room and the parlour door shut behind him. 'Hello,' murmured the new arrival.

'Good afternoon,' replied a politely but stiffly smiling Anna.

With a round-shouldered, clumsy gait, Mr Sleighman made his way towards her. She resisted the urge to climb up onto the highest table in the room, and instead kept a china-doll smile fixed on her face.

Upon reaching her, he placed on her lips a hesitant and bumbling but eager kiss. She did not kiss him back. The roughness of the small patch just above his mouth he had missed in shaving rasped harshly against her lip. She almost stepped back.

He seemed to have noticed her frowning face and rigid body. 'Sorry...' he murmured, moving his face past hers.

She swept over to the large bay windows and looked out.

He padded cautiously after her. 'How're you?'

'I remain well. And how are you?'

'Good...good... Sorry I was late. I'm not usually late...'

She felt a stab of conscience. The heat might have given her a slight headache and a significant moodiness, but it was not fair to be mean to poor Mr Sleighman. He really was trying his best. A young lady must always be nice to people no matter what—unless they were Russian, of course.

Anna coaxed the china-doll smile back into place. 'Did you have a satisfactory morning?'

He seated himself in the chair she had indicated. 'Yes. I worked on my sermon and then paid a visit to Dean Station...'

Although her face smiled and nodded, Mr Sleighman's quiet tones soon faded from Anna's ears as her mind wandered off. She found herself mulling on the particulars of the reverend's features. He looked far too boyish for his thirty-five years. He was slightly built and shorter than her, even though she herself was only a little above average height for a woman. His hair was dark and close-cropped. The thought that it was also coarse and wiry presented itself to her, but she killed it. Dark and close-cropped. Anything else would just not be nice, and she was a nice girl. The skin was swarthy. Very practical in such a sunny climate. The bone structure was reasonably pleasing, although it lacked a certain refinement; the forehead was heavy, and the chin rather long and weak. The eyes were light brown—when one could see them, which was not often. Mr Sleighman tended not to look one in the eye when he was speaking to one. Like the way he was looking over her head and out the window at this very moment.

The lips. Perhaps she was not quite so nice today. The top lip looked well enough. But the bottom lip. The bottom lip was too full, too engorged. It reminded her of a brown pear that had become over-ripe and was on the verge of decay. The sort of pear one sometimes innocently closes one's hand around only to one's finger sinking into browned, slimy mushiness. Today she was truly vile. Then there was the nose. The nose did not bear thinking about.

She moved her attention onto the large fly monotonously, lazily, droning about overhead. She eyed it intently, willing the offending insect to settle somewhere within reach so she could squash it. But the lazy, monotonous droning just went on. And on. And on.

Gritting her teeth, she moved her eyes onto the view out the window. The bright blue sea shimmered and sparkled in the sunlight beating down on it. It seemed so happy, so playful. As if the waters were laughing with joy. What did the ocean know that she did not? What happy secret was it concealing from her?

Presently, the tea things were brought in and placed on the low table in the centre of the room. Fine china platters piled with cheese and cucumber club sandwiches, scones, teacakes and ladyfinger biscuits accompanied the finest tea set of bone china.

A pity her appetite had quite left her by now.

She reached over to pour the tea. Mr Sleighman reached over too. Her reluctance to give the task up was matched by his determination to take it over. Each with a hand on the teapot, they poured the tea out. Almost as much tea found itself on the tray as in the cups while the teapot was wrestled over. He beat her to the sugar. She gave a little sigh as two lumps instead of one were deposited in her cup. Six months and still he did not remember. While he was busy with the sugar, she took the chance to seize the milk jug. But her victory was not complete. Mr Sleighman still insisted on putting his hand over hers as the milk was poured. A grimace escaped her, but it was too late. There was already far too much milk in her tea.

Holding her cup in bitterly tight fingers, she took a pinched little sip. And set the cup back down. Did he think her so feeble and helpless she could not even make tea without his help, or did he merely believe he could do everything better than she? Well, he couldn't. The tea was foul.

She took a deep breath. What had got into her today? Mr Sleighman was only being gentlemanly. He merely wished to help.

Mr Sleighman appeared to have sensed Anna's displeasure. He frowned worriedly across at her. 'I really think people are often too critical of their spouse. Always wanting them to change, always wanting them to be perfect.'

She regarded him sourly over the tea things. Vagueness and inaccuracy annoyed her. Why did he not say 'you' instead of 'people' and 'me' in place of 'their spouse'? For that was what he truly meant. Because he was criticising her.

'I would not wish anyone to change themselves just for *me*,' she replied coldly. 'The betterment of one's character is a moral duty, not a favour to others.'

Mr Sleighman cleared his throat and narrowed his eyes at her in the way he always did when he was about to flatter her. 'You look beautiful today—you look beautiful *every* day.'

She snapped a ladyfinger biscuit in half. He only ever said things like that when he suspected she was cross with him. 'Thank you.' Her tone was flat and emotionless.

Being complimented by him meant little to her. She really was far out of his league. He may well be a bishop one day, but at present, he was merely a lowly vicar. Moreover, he was completely desperate to marry. Even more desperate than she.

A stiff silence reigned for a while before Mr Sleighman spoke again. 'If you say five hundred things to a woman, she will only remember the one bad thing you said and forget the other four hundred and ninety-nine good things.'

Anna carefully placed the piece of biscuit into her mouth and slowly, deliberately, sunk her teeth into it. The man could be such a chicken. Why did he not ask what he really wanted to?

She over-carefully wiped away the crumbs at the corners of her lips. 'Do you mean to tell me, Mr Sleighman, that you believe women are unforgiving and lacking in generosity?'

He wilted like a weed in the midday sun beneath the grim glare she had fixed on him. 'No, not at all! When God created woman, I believe he gave them all the best qualities! A woman has emotions and sensitivities which a man can't feel. She is able to do so many things at once—mind the children, instruct the maids, organise the cooking in kitchen, while a man just sits and reads the paper.'

Anna looked at him with a face that was as unreadable as a blank page. 'If, as you claim, God created the man and this laziness and coldness were a part of his being before the fall, I really do hope you can provide me with a postal address at which I might reach Him, for I heartily desire to write to Him and complain.'

Mr Sleighman almost spilt his tea. 'Anna, you—you don't understand my meaning correctly! While a woman has some nice emotional qualities, she lacks the rational mind God has endowed the man with. Difficult theological questions are beyond her mental faculties.'

Anna did not reply. She instead carefully placed the second half of the ladyfinger biscuit into her mouth and bit down hard.

Mr Sleighman was of course right, she told herself. The weaker sex are indeed scatty-minded, over-emotional creatures. Strange then that she was nearly always so calm, so cold, so emotionally reserved. The only time she had ever cried in front of someone was on that hot summer's day in the park beneath the spreading elm tree. That day when Sasha Ivanovsky came to her...the silver-maned Russian with his heavy-lidded dark eyes and sad, tender smile—what was wrong with her!

She started to her feet and almost knocked the tea tray off the table. Giving the startled Mr Sleighman a reassuring little smile that she hoped did not look as forced as it felt, she walked over to the window.

A good thing indeed that the Tree of Knowledge was not in the vicinity. A mood like this could have invented sin out of sheer boredom. Mr Sleighman was a respectable man. An upstanding Christian. A man of good family. She did not love him, of course.

But that was not relevant. All sensible people said that love came after marriage. You simply chose a good match and decided you were going to make it work.

'Are you alright, Anna?' came the reverend's cautious inquiry.

'It is merely the heat which is making me feel rather strained. I am afraid my head aches somewhat.'

'Would you like to take a walk around the lawn? The breeze might be cooling.'

She nodded weakly. Mr Sleighman hurried over to offer her his arm an order to escort her outside. She took the offered arm reluctantly, as she disliked standing this close to him. Being taller than her escort made her feel unfeminine and lacking in daintiness.

They exited the house. The breeze outside was indeed cooling. The way Mr Sleighman put his arm around her waist was not. Her head ached more. Mr Sleighman moved in closer. The hand moved below her waist. She felt stickier than ever. Once they had passed out of sight of the house windows, he put his other hand on her breast.

'Mr Sleighman!' she gasped, angrily pushing him away. Then she continued walking down towards the seashore in loud silence.

'Sorry...' she heard his murmured apology trailing after her.

She turned around. But Mr Sleighman was already slinking back to the house like a dog with its tail between its legs.

She stumbled on. That was the problem with Mr Sleighman. He begged and jumped and salivated about her like a hungry dog at her feet waiting while its dinner is being prepared. Every time he looked at her he practically had his tongue hanging out, and he was forever pushing his luck. Every time she beat him down he slunk off like he had just now. But like a scolded dog, he always came creeping back to his mistress's feet and before long he was trying again. It made her feel like a piece of meat with a fly circling about it.

When Anna reached the beach, she passed through the sand dunes until she came to a log washed up at the high tide line. She sunk down onto it.

The tide was at its lowest and the sea seemed strangely still, filled with the expectant hush of a theatre audience in the moments before the curtain goes up on an eagerly awaited drama. Far out on the horizon, a gathering of dark indigo storm clouds brooded over the glassy waters.

Anna drew her wandering impressions back to her own inner state. She had no right to be unhappy, no right at all. She had everything: wealth, youth, friends, family, a devoted fiancé, respectability. Yet her life seemed so pointless and empty.

She looked down at the long, trailing hem of her favourite lavender gown. It was covered in dirt.

Without warning, she suddenly burst into tears and, alone with the gulls and the whispering waters, just sat there and cried and cried and cried. And just when the sobs seemed to be abating, a fresh wave of grief flooded over her and the tears sprung afresh.

* * * *

By sundown, storm clouds filled the twilit sky. It was as though a swarming host of gods on the warpath had swept in overhead. Darkness fell early. The boom of thunder rolled forth like the echo of racing chariots and charging horses. With a low moan that increased to a furious howl in one breath, the wind sprung up from nowhere. It was the divine war band's battle cry, and the lightning forking across the inky darkness their flashing spears.

Anna watched the battle raging in the skies over Gravemore with fearful awe. The ocean joined forces with the heavenly war band, and the furious pounding roar of wave after wave charging the beach like rows of cavalry sounded from the shore.

She felt a strange excitement take hold of her. The thundering roar of this ride of the Valkyrie passing overhead awakened an intense wakefulness deep within. It felt as if the storm's electricity flowed through her own body.

As she watched from her dark upstairs bedroom, the inky war band at last rolled off to the southwest, leaving the full moon's serene silver orb smiling secretively down on the tossing, foaming waters below.

Suddenly, another light shining forth from the darkness caught her eye. One moment there was nothing, the next a light was violently pitching in the blackness just off the cape.

Her heart started violently. It was a ship. A ship had rounded the cape close to shore. Much too close to shore. Much too close to the reef stretching out from the cape. In a sea like this, a ship would be pounded to matchsticks on the jagged rocks in moments.

A heartbeat later she was running downstairs crying, 'A ship, a ship is being wrecked on the reef!'

Soon she and the station's farmhands were running down to the seashore.

When she reached water's edge, the roar of the waves was

deafening and the howling gale pulled at her skirts as if determined to tear them from her. In the dim light offered by the moon, she stared at the raging ocean in panic. What now? She felt disorientated in the turmoil.

'A boat! I see a small boat surfing in on the breakers!' shouted one of the men, pointing directly ahead.

She looked. An overturned rowing boat was being blown to shore by the gale. Several figures could just be seen clinging desperately to their lifeboat.

The farmhands rushed into the foaming waves to help pull the boat to shore. Seeing that these shipwrecked mariners were safe, Anna decided to walk up the beach towards the reef, where she could hear the crashing groans of the ship grinding against the rocks.

Someone might have washed up closer to the wreck. But the chances of them surviving the pounding anyone would receive as they passed over the reef meant she was looking for corpses rather than survivors.

Fighting at every step the gale that seemed determined to push her back down the beach, Anna moved closer to the cape. She scanned the foaming sea. What was that white shape lying in the shallows?

She ran towards it, then suddenly stopped. It was a body lying face down. A man dressed in a white shirt. He could not be alive, for he had silver hair. An older man would never make it through the furious breakers and pitiless rocks alive. She dreaded coming any closer. She might see things—things that would sicken her, because this corpse was certain to have been battered and broken.

A finger moved.

Anna almost screamed.

Then a hand moved.

Anna ran over and flung herself to her knees beside the body in the shallow water. 'Sir, sir, are you injured?'

A faint groan reached her ears.

Then she noticed dark blood on the side of the man's head. 'Does it hurt anywhere else—broken limbs and such like?' she demanded breathlessly, seizing him by the shoulders.

'What dream is this...?' the shipwrecked one gasped weakly.

'You are not dreaming; I am quite real. You are safe now.'

'But Anya appears to me only in my dreams...'

She frowned. 'Anya?'

Then her heart suddenly jumped into her throat. Anya! She was Anya! And he was—she pulled his shoulder so he rolled onto his back.

3

If Only Words Could Convey

SASHA Ivanovsky's soulful brown eyes met hers swimmingly, their focus uncertain and distant. Then he weakly lifted a dripping hand and reached slowly up to touch her face. 'What strange bliss is this, what happy vision...?'

It could not be, it could not be! She stared. She put her hand over her mouth. She let it fall again. She opened her mouth, but although her lips moved, no sound came out.

She could not see him again. Could not.

His icy, wonder-filled hand moved slowly over her cold cheek. 'Oh, happy, blessed day...'

She shook her head. 'No. No.'

The full, sensitive lips melted into that sad, unbearably tender smile which had hovered on the edge of her mind, in the depths of her dreams, every day since the ball.

Something hard and cold in her heart started to melt too. She desperately looked away across the raging sea. 'No, no, no!'

The anguished scream was devoured by the howling gale in an instant.

She looked again at the water-soaked white figure lying beside her on the wet sand as the foaming waves lapped around him. The frigid hand covering her cheek faded in strength, and the half-open eyes grew more distant. Slowly the hand fell limply down onto his chest and the eyes flickered like a candle flame before an extinguishing draft, then fell shut.

A terror she had never felt before seized her heart. She shook him with all the strength she possessed. 'Sasha, Sasha, wake up!'

But his frigid body was limp and unresponsive to her furious panic. Almost blind with fear, she leaned down low over his face and put a finger to his neck. Yes, his heart was still beating. But no breath of his warmed her cheek.

She shook him violently again. 'Sasha, don't go, don't leave me!'

The body remained cold and silent. The only movement came from the wind tossing the wet silver strands of hair about the deathly pale face. Anna's arms burned with the effort of shaking the unyielding weight of his body.

'Wake up, you selfish bastard!' She screamed with the little breath left in her, and slapped his white cheek.

His head fell limply to one side, so that his other cheek now rested on the damp sand.

Anna's fear-filled rage suddenly drained from her. Sasha did not need any more of her anguish and brutality. No, he needed love, he needed warmth, he needed life. And she had these things. It was time to cease being a miser and share them with the man who was dying for lack of them. After all, he would not even have been sailing the angry seas if she had not forced him to cut short his stay in Auckland.

She placed a gentle hand upon his brow and turned his face back towards her. Then she took a deep breath, leaned forward and put her mouth to his parted blue lips. Their touch was icy and death-like. Anna quickly moved her hand down to his press his nostrils together and breathed out all of her breath.

A weak groan reached her ears above the howl of the gale and angry crash of sea flinging itself against boulder. But he did not open his eyes.

Anna breathed another long breath into his body. When she lifted her lips from his, a faint warmth brushed softly against her cheek. Hardly daring to hope, she paused and waited. And there it was again. His warm breath on her cold cheek.

She let her exhausted head drop onto his chest. 'Thank you, oh God, thank you…' she whispered.

'You found another one!'

Anna looked up to find one of the farmhands hurrying towards her through the windy darkness. 'Yes, please help! He is senseless and quite weak.'

* * * *

It could not be—it *must* not be. This could not be happening. It was not fair. After all that effort trying to forget. Trying to forget those eyes so like a darkened forest. That divine smile. That mysterious earthly yet heavenly beauty. That shock of silver hair which shone like pristine snow beneath starlight.

Anna turned from the open window and resumed pacing up and down her moonlit bedroom.

She was so near to her wedding day, so near to safety. It was less than two weeks to go. After that there would not, *could* not, be any more wild thoughts and strange moods threatening to destroy her life as she knew it. She would be safe from the sea's siren song forever, safely joined to the Reverend Sleighman in wedlock. Mr Sleighman had neither the brain nor the verve to think dangerous thoughts. Lucky wretch. A year or two under his hand and neither would she.

But forgetting Sasha Ivanovsky for even a second was impossible, a hopeless task she had been toiling at all night. It was impossible when the man himself lay in the room right next to her own. Thoughts of him flooded every corner of her being. Emotions that terrified her filled her heart. The sound of his voice resounded in her ears. The feel of his shivering hand would not leave her fevered cheek however much she slapped it.

She threw herself down on her unslept-in bed and waited for morning.

The thought of the new day brought on a fresh flood of anguish. What would Ivanovsky say when he finally regained full consciousness? Would everyone at Gravemore discover her shameful little secret? She barely prevented herself from falling onto the floor and curling up into a ball.

Nevertheless, of one thing there was no doubt. She would avoid Ivanovsky at all costs.

* * * *

At eight O'clock in the morning, the doctor arrived at Gravemore. Anna waited in her room until her sister Jennifer had shown the good doctor up to the patient's bedroom. She waited until she heard the door close behind Dr Bramell and Jennifer's always-hurrying footsteps disappearing back down the stairs, then ventured out like a mouse leaving its hole. She glided silently up to the closed door next to her own and put her ear to the keyhole.

'So old chap, nothing broken, eh?' came the doctor's jovial tones.

'No,' Ivanovsky replied quietly. 'But this knock to the head does seem to have brought some strange illusions with it.'

'What are we talking here?'

'When I washed up on the beach, I fancied a lady from my past came and spoke to me.'

'Ha ha ha!' The doctor's jolly laugh rang forth. 'Well well, you young chaps do tend to get into quite a flap about some belle or other from time to time. Having fantasies about ladies is quite natural for a young man.'

'I suppose you are right,' sighed Ivanovsky. 'Although it did seem so real. I touched her cheek, and I could have sworn she was there...'

'By jingo, ha ha ha! I would not fret, old chap. The mind is good at playing tricks on its unsuspecting owner. When the head receives a hard knock, well, it is just like dropping a fine machine; things get shaken up a bit.'

The thoughtful 'hmmm' Ivanovsky gave in reply sounded unconvinced, but he said no more.

Anna made out the sound of the doctor putting things back into his bag. 'Jolly good then. Keep to your bed for a couple of days. Might sound like humbug, but it will do you good. I will call on you again tomorrow. Toodle-pip.'

Then Dr Bramell's steps approached the door.

The breathlessly listening Anna darted back into her room. Thank *God*. She was safe—for now.

* * * *

Anna told the maid who came to put her room in order that she was feeling too unwell to come down for breakfast, so would be spending the morning in her room. Nervous exhaustion and a headache brought on by the cold from being out on the beach last night were provided as the reason.

Her head felt fine. However, the nervous exhaustion was true. She could not face any of her relatives, or worse still, Mr Sleighman. She was in no mood for exchanging polite nothings and pretending to find their conversation interesting, and was terrified someone might notice that she was seething with emotions she had no right to be feeling.

The maid returned with breakfast and the latest Gravemore morning news bulletin, hot off the tongue. The ship was the *Spirit*, a small coastal vessel that carried goods and passengers between New Zealand's coastal towns. All of the *Spirit*'s seven crew and one passenger had survived. It had been sailing from Napier to Wellington. The crew had all made it safely to shore with the lifeboat. The passenger disappeared down below in a desperate search for his baggage, which he would not leave without when the order to abandon ship was given. The captain and crew abandoned ship anyway. After spending the night in the shearers' quarters, the *Spirit*'s crew had left by horse and cart for Waipawa, the nearest town. There they intended to board the stagecoach to Napier. The passenger was going to wait for the ship which, within the next two weeks, would be stopping off Aramoana Beach and sending a rowing boat ashore to collect the station's baled wool clip.

Anna was then left in peace to chew this information over along with her morning toast with marmalade, scrambled eggs and halved grapefruit. It was washed down with tea containing one sugar lump and just a dash of milk. In other words, tea that was blessedly free from Mr Sleighman's touch.

Later she had luncheon brought up to her room too. However, when the time came around at which she usually took her daily walk, she decided to attempt to slip out the back entrance unnoticed. Firmly tying her bonnet on and putting a shawl around her shoulders to ward off the strong, cool easterly breeze blowing in from the sea, she gingerly set off down the hallway.

The stairs were negotiated without incident. She passed the open dining room door. Nothing happened. She crept past the parlour door. Again nothing untoward happened. She began to breathe a little easier.

She neared the kitchen door. It suddenly flew open in her face and there stood Aunt Day the housekeeper.

Anna panicked. Even though she was only a servant, Aunt Day had somehow succeeded in cowing Anna into mute terror right from the day she arrived.

'Kindly take this up to the patient.'

She stared at the tray the housekeeper held out. No, it could not be happening—

'Well, don't just stand there like a deaf mute!'

Anna looked up to Aunt Day's sharp-nosed little face. 'But I was just about to go out for my walk. Could not one of the maids—'

'Do not argue with me, young lady! Now off you go with this upstairs.'

'But—'

'Ah, no more!' The tray was thrust into Anna's hands and Aunt Day retreated back down her lair before Anna could utter another word of protest.

Anna stared down at the tray of tea and chicken soup in horror. Then suddenly she relaxed. Of course: she would find one of the maids upstairs and get her to do it.

Anna briskly climbed the stairs. When she reached the top, she placed the tray down on the hall table. Then she searched the bedrooms one by one. Empty. Empty. Empty. Empty. And empty.

She stopped searching for a maid and started searching for a new plan instead. As she chewed her lip thoughtfully, she looked at the door before her in fearful vexation.

She thought for a good while. Then she slowly nodded to herself as a plan at last came to her. Yes...a disguise...a disguise might work...

She put her shawl over her head and pulled it close down so it covered most of her face. Then she softly knocked on the door, while her knees loudly knocked against each other.

'Come in.'

She slowly opened the door and, with eyes fixed on the floor, scuttled desperately towards the bedside table. Her hands shook with such violence that a din loud enough to wake the dead emanated from the tray as the cups, plates, spoons and tea things danced a merry jig across its surface.

With her mouth a twist of pure pain, she shoved the tray onto the table.

'Thank you, *babushka*,' Ivanovsky murmured.

Anna just turned and dived for the open door with a speed that would have killed any real grandmother.

Her hands were still shaking when she reached the seashore.

Aunt Day could be such a menace with her organising, busybody ways. Anna found herself wishing far more often than was polite that Aunt Day would drop dead.

Had he noticed? It seemed he had not, but his suspicions surely had been aroused. A good thing that the laughing doctor never really listened to his patients' complaints and believed everything was merely a trick of the brain.

She was alongside the reef at the southern end of the bay before she even realised she was walking there. The wooden wreckage that littered the high-water mark at the centre and northern end of the beach was almost absent from here.

But something half-submerged in the shallows caught her eye. A wave would carry the thing almost to shore, then drag it back out. She stood at the waterline willing the thing, which appeared to be an item of luggage, to beach. The sea just kept playing with it like a kitten toying with a ball. Back and forth, back and forth, the waves swept it.

With a huff of annoyance at the uncooperative waves, Anna lifted her voluminous skirts high and waded out to the trunk bobbing in the sea. The prize was seized and carried to shore.

There, she set her treasure haul down and frowned at it. Another of those pesky puzzles. A label caught her eye. But unfortunately, some of the letters written on the leather suitcase's label sticker had washed or worn off. She frowned harder as she read the letters: I NO SKY.

I no sky? What on earth did it mean?

She frowned and puzzled some more. Then she yelped aloud. Ivanovsky! It read Ivanovsky!

No wonder she did not like puzzles. Anyone this bad at them was sure not to.

The humble, battered trunk suddenly took on the aura of an object of magic, mystical, maybe-holy-maybe-evil qualities. She carefully removed her hands from it and stepped back to gaze at it in awed silence. Then she gently lifted it, tucked it beneath her shawl and turned for home.

Anna succeeded in smuggling the booty up to her bedroom without being intercepted. Once the door was safely shut, she set it down on her desk, then sat herself down on the edge of her bed and stared at it. And stared at it. And stared at it some more. The trunk almost blushed.

Then she opened the chest at the bottom of her bed, lifted one of the piles of corsets and undergarments filling it, dumped the suitcase in and slammed the lid shut.

And only just in time, for a moment later a knock sounded on her door.

'Yes?'

'N, it is Jennifer. Might I come in?'

'Yes, do come,' said Anna. But not before she had grimaced crossly. She hated the pet name inexplicably bestowed on her by her sisters.

Jennifer stuck her head around the door. 'I came to inquire as to whether we are to expect you for dinner? Mr Sleighman is coming over. He will be frightfully disappointed if you insist on moping about up here.'

Anna felt her brow with a suitably feeble hand. 'I am terribly afraid, Jen, that I shall not be able to grace your little dinner party with my company tonight. This *malaise* is still with me. I am wretchedly tired—and I am not moping!'

Jennifer regarded her sister with narrowed eyes and a slight harshness. 'N, it is not like you to be sulking about like this. I know how much you detest sentimental nonsense and feeble-minded mooning around.'

Anna put a pillow over her head. 'Jen, I really am quite unwell, and if you continue plaguing me in this manner I shall think you dreadfully cruel.'

Jennifer let out an annoyed sigh. 'I shall desist in that case. But you know how much Mr Sleighman adores hearing you sing after dinner. The poor man will be quite inconsolable when I tell him you would not come down.'

Anna turned her back on her sister and pulled the pillow more tightly around her head.

Jennifer waited for Anna to speak again.

But Anna was far too busy cringing to even consider saying anything. Singing! She could not bear to even think about it. As if there was not enough horror and wretchedness to be found in life without being cajoled into singing.

Jennifer gave up and left Anna to her agonies.

Once Jennifer's steps had faded, Anna removed the pillow from her head. Then she silently lay on the bed. And the suitcase just quietly lay in the chest. But the suitcase weighed on Anna's mind so much that it might as well have been lying on her head.

She was burning to know what was inside it. To know what it was that Ivanovsky could not bear to leave behind on the stricken ship. The mere thought of rifling through a gentleman's private possessions filled the polite, proper part of her with shame and horror. But the Anna buried somewhere deep beneath that was less inhibited. This Anna was hated and repressed by the other one, but the thought that the untamed Anna would be locked away in a dark mausoleum forever when she became Mrs Sleighman made her strangely wild. What would be the harm?

She slowly approached the chest. After a final furtive look around, she lifted its lid. The case was seized and laid onto her dressing table. Feeling like a burglar, she undid the buckle and slowly, slowly lifted the lid.

Inside was a bundle wrapped in oilcloth. Cords held it tightly together. She tried to untie them but could not. She argued with them until her fingertips were red and smarting. Then she did something she knew she should not: she took her sewing scissors and cut them. She unwrapped the package with the anticipation of a child on Christmas morning.

But still her goal eluded her, for the package was wrapped in yet another piece of oilcloth. When she cut the cord this time, she had no polite reservations. Bad behaviour quickly made friends with bored misery.

A moment later brushes, tubes of paint and palettes tumbled out onto the dressing table. Then another oilcloth-wrapped package dropped on top. She pulled at the ribbon encircling it, which fell smoothly open. Inside was a roll of thick paper sheets. With one swipe of her arm, she shoved everything else off the tabletop.

Then Anna carefully unrolled the large paper sheets. And there, gazing up at her with solemn grey eyes, was Anna herself.

She sprung back as though she had been stung. From the other side of the room, she regarded the painting with an expression more suited to one faced by an angry rhinoceros than a sheet of paper and pigment. Her heart raced and her cheeks felt strangely numb. What did it *mean*? Why had he painted a lady he had met only twice? Why did he keep it with him, and so carefully protected against the damp too?

It had never even occurred to her that Ivanovsky might have seen her as more than a pleasant night at the ball, a pleasant face to look at, a pleasant fancy to amuse one's self with while in town. She had not doubted that he had long since forgotten her.

Like someone approaching a wild animal, Anna slowly crept back over to her dressing table. She dared to look upon the painting once again. He had painted her dressed in the violet-blue dress she had worn at the ball. The painted Anna leaned nonchalantly against a white Grecian pillar, her face turned towards the viewer. In a graceful hand a pink rose was carelessly held, and soft light flooded down from above.

The young lady meeting Anna's eyes so boldly was her. But yet it was not. The eyes were the same grey. However, the painted eyes were filled with life and vitality, while the eyes that stared back at her from the dressing table mirror were dull, dead and hollow. The painted figure was lithe and graceful, while she felt stiff and rigid. The painted mouth was decided and bold, while the one in the mirror was tight with unspoken misery.

If Ivanovsky fancied himself in love with her, then the woman he loved did not really exist. All such love was an illusion, she told herself. People talked of love when, if they were truly honest, they should have been talking about money, and about their own needs and desires. It annoyed her that men felt they had to pretend that they loved a woman when really they did not. Like Mr Sleighman.

He pretended, but all he really wanted was someone to nurture him, bear his children and satisfy his carnal desires.

She glided over to the open window and looked out on the gathering twilight. To be fair, though, Sasha Ivanovsky had always behaved in a selfless and gentlemanly manner. He had not badgered her or made demands on her, and he had done exactly as she asked.

Anna flung herself down on the window seat. Having not slept since the night before last, her eyelids drooped and her head started to nod. The cool night air was calming, the chirp of the grass-crickets soothing, and the heavy, milky sweetness of the jasmine scrambling up the house wall drowsily captivating. The distant cry of a morepork owl drifted across on the soft darkness.

When Anna was about to allow herself to be gently lulled to sleep by the music of the night, a new song quietly joined the night's peaceful chorus. It came from the window of the room next to her own. A clear, pure tenor voice singing a Russian folk song with a melancholy, slowly rising and falling melody. The song was simple, yet everything that was profound, deep and beautiful was contained within it. It was a reverential prayer to nature in music. A tribute to suffering. A gathering up of every heartfelt longing that had ever filled a soul. A thing both profoundly sad and profoundly beautiful.

Anna listened entranced. The song and its purely beautiful melody embodied the vague longing that had tormented her for so long. It poured into her emptiness. A peace she had never known before descended on her. It flowed into her heart and wrapped itself about her.

No more was she tormented, no more…

The golden voice poured forth song after heavenly song, each as sad, prayerful and beautiful as the last. It seemed as though a cathedral dedicated to the worship of nature arose in the lustrous darkness. A cathedral built of music.

Anna worshiped at its altar with utter reverence, and eventually the singer carried her off into sleep on a bed of heavenly peace.

* * * *

Anna pressed her ear close against the keyhole and held her breath.

'How are you feeling this morning, old chap?'

'I feel well. But these strange visions, still they haunt me.'

'Indeed?'

'*Oui.* Yesterday a stooped old woman brought my food up, and although I saw her face hardly at all, somehow I fancied her to be girl from my past.'

'Ha ha ha!' The doctor's laugh contained a touch of unease, as if he was not sure if it was he or his patient who was mad. 'You mistook a granny for a young girl? By jingo, ha ha ha!'

'Yes, some unmistakeable likeness was there.' Ivanovsky sounded slightly annoyed.

'Ha ha ha! By jingo, that knock to the head really has done some damage. Here, take some of this laudanum. It will help you sleep.'

'Sleep comes to me without reluctance.' Ivanovsky sounded quite put out.

'Just take it anyway, old chap. Can't do you any harm, I daresay. Ha ha ha!'

'I do not want it.'

'Very good, just stay in bed for a few more days then. Ha ha ha! Toodle-pip, old chap.'

Suddenly the door opened. Anna was face-to-face with the white-whiskered, red-faced doctor. They stared at each other in surprise for a moment.

Then the doctor laughed. 'Ha ha ha!'

But the laugh did little to disguise the fluster Ivanovsky had put him in. The laughing doctor clearly did not like to be puzzled either.

Anna stepped back. 'Do pardon me, I was just passing.'

To her great relief, the doctor shut the door behind him. 'Miss Annette, I believe?'

Her mouth lifted into a smile of relief. 'Yes, that is right.'

'Your sister informed me, my dear, that you have been suffering with your nerves?'

By now, she had succeeded in leading the doctor almost to the top of the stairs. 'That is correct. The preparations for the wedding have left me quite fraught, and the shipwreck…'

'Ha ha ha! No need to say anymore, my dear.' He patted her patronisingly on the arm and gave her a knowing wink. 'Every new bride can do with a little help. Ha ha ha!' He placed a bottle in her hand and was gone.

She looked down. It was a large bottle of laudanum.

Excellent. She was down to her last few sips. But her relief was quickly disturbed by unease. What had started out as a little relief for a bad cold two years ago had grown into something of a regular habit. The things she told herself—that it was medicine for her headaches and anxiety—had started to wear thin now that she often took a sip despite feeling in perfectly normal health. The way Ivanovsky had determinedly, almost rudely, refused the laudanum reminded her that there was little difference between what she was doing and what the poor wretches who frequented opium dens did.

But you got yours from a doctor, squeaked the little opium-loving demon in her mind.

'Yes, this laudanum is medicine,' she whispered aloud. 'I am not addicted to it. I need it for my health.'

* * * *

Feeling safe in the knowledge that Ivanovsky had been ordered to keep to his bed for a few more days, Anna decided to venture out into the garden later that morning. But just in case, she took the precaution of putting on her widest-brimmed bonnet and wrapping a thick veil around it. Then, fearing she might be spotted from an upstairs window, she took a parasol before making her way out the door.

The fresh sea air was most invigorating after so much time spent hiding indoors, and the green lawn delightfully springy under foot. Moreover, the novel in her hand and bottle of laudanum in her pocket promised an enjoyable few hours spent wandering around the garden and lounging on the seat beneath the shady pergola.

Anna unfurled her parasol and opened *Sense and Sensibility* as she slowly drifted along the lawn towards the paved path leading into the walled herb garden with the pergola.

When she reached page thirty-two, where Miss Marianne

Dashwood was holding forth on the youthfulness of amour, her pace slowed.

A woman of seven-and-twenty can never hope to feel or inspire affection again.

Anna stopped. She was seven-and-twenty. The condemned one stared at the page in mute horror. Could it really be true?

She lifted her eyes from the page and stared unseeingly out over the ocean. Surely not? But in her heart she felt that Marianne was right. A woman of her years had no business with love. The joys of youth had passed her by in the night unseen. Now only a cold, grey dawn of misery remained. Never would she be the tender young maiden whose face delighted a lover's dark eyes, never would hers be the tiny fingers whose hesitant touch on a cheek set a manly heart racing…

Thank goodness for laudanum.

She sighed and returned mournfully to her book. But no sooner were her eyes on the page, when she lifted them again with a start. The sound of footsteps was approaching.

Mr Sleighman? No, the tread was much too confident, much too decided and heavy. Her nerves took flight like a flock of startled birds. With a racing heart, she lifted her skirts and looked franticly about. The house? No, that would mean going towards the footsteps. The paddock? No, there was no gate here; climbing over the fence would be horribly slow. The herb garden? Yes.

4

When, My Soul, You Wanted

ANNA started to run. But the heel of her right shoe became caught between a crack in the paving stones. Before she even had time to think about what she was doing, she had abandoned the shoe to its fate and was limping into the herb garden. As soon as she reached the seat, she flung herself down, opened her book and stuck her heavily veiled face in it. She prayed the footsteps would not follow.

The slow, measured tread paused at about the place she had lost her shoe. She could hardly bear to listen. Then it moved on.

Closer and closer came the footsteps. They were in the herb garden now. He—for it had to be a he—would have seen her by now. The footsteps came right up to her. Then they stopped. She flinched.

'Miss Cinderella, I presume?'

The voice was Ivanovsky's. Anna could tell he was almost

laughing.

She shrunk into the corner of the seat and resolutely refused to look up from her book. 'No,' she replied in an Irish accent. 'She most likely has left by pumpkin-coach. Go and look for the tracks on the driveway.'

Lucky thing she had always had a talent for imitating the speech of others. The Irish maid at Elton Towers had given Anna plenty of opportunities, and she was confident her voice would not give her away.

A low laugh greeted this reply. 'I retrieved your glass slipper from the path. It must have fallen off as you fled.'

She had to grip the book firmly to stop it shaking. 'I am missing nothing.'

'Pardon my insolence, Miss Cinderella, but I believe you not.'

She almost gave in to the compelling desire to look up at the tenderly teasing smile she was certain he was wearing. At that moment, she would have given almost anything for one glance at Sasha Ivanovsky's divinely loving face. Anything except her respectability and elevated position in society.

Consoling herself with the thought of the laudanum awaiting her forgetfulness-seeking lips, she brutally forced her head to remain down. 'Sir, I have everything.'

He laughed. The sound was filled with such genuine good humour that she felt like crying.

'Seeing as you have neither dovecote nor pear tree to hide from your prince in, Miss Cinderella, I shall take liberty of insisting you prove that claim.'

Anna felt ridiculous. What on earth must he think of a lady so rude she refused to look at the gentleman speaking to her even once?

She presented her shod foot with what she hoped was enough briefness to ensure he would not notice it was the left foot.

He laughed his low, burnished laugh again. 'It is unfortunate for you that I am not as easily fooled as prince in tale. For instance, I happen to possess knowledge of fact that ladies generally do not have two left feet.'

Some may have found such an unusual predicament rather amusing. Anna did not. She cringed with complete humiliation. Behaving in a manner considered less than proper was almost unthinkable. Blushing furiously beneath her thick veil, she presented the left foot's naked twin.

He dropped to his knee before her. The scent of cologne engulfed her senses. Her throat felt as though iron hands gripped it. Her rigid body trembled slightly with the desperate effort it took to force herself not to bolt like a startled rabbit.

A large, soft hand closed gently but firmly around her fearfully shrinking foot. A little gasp escaped her lips as his warmth seeped into her cold skin.

'Allow me to reunite lost friends.'

As usual, his presence felt so intimate, and as usual, Anna was terrified by such feelings. It felt as though his warm, gentle hands had closed around her very soul. As though he held her beating heart in his loving hands.

He appeared to take her silence as assent. The pink satin slipper was ever so carefully eased into place.

'There, Cinderella no longer is half-shod,' came his announcement, once the shoe was on.

She could almost see Sasha's unbearably beautiful smile through the brim of her bonnet. For she knew that was what he was doing at that moment. Even though she had spent less than twelve hours in his company, she felt as though she could read his mind. As he knelt before her, he was wishing the mysterious lady was not so ashamed of her facial disfigurement that she could not bear to be looked upon by a stranger.

'Thank you, you are kind,' she whispered, almost forgetting to put on the Irish accent.

A gentle hand touched her arm. 'Cinderella is ready for the ball now.'

Then a terrible thing happened. A wicked, puckish gust of wind suddenly jumped up from nowhere and snatched the bonnet clean off Anna's head in the blink of an eye.

She let out a scream of terror and brought her arms up to her face as she franticly turned away. But it was too late.

'Anya!' cried Ivanovsky.

She had to get away. It was her only thought.

With her hands clutched to her face as though it was on fire, Anna leapt up. But as she took a blindly panicked step forward, she stumbled on the open parasol left lying beside the garden seat. Before her mind could catch up, she hit the hard flagstones with a shattering smash. She lay where she fell; face down, staring at the cold, mossy stones.

He was kneeling beside her in an instant. 'Good God! Anya, are you hurt?'

'I am perfectly fine,' she said numbly, still refusing to look up. Her knees and elbows throbbed with pain.

'But blood, it is all over your leg!'

With her head down, she miserably pulled her herself into a sitting position. There was nowhere to hide or run now. Dead fatalism replaced fear. 'It is not blood.'

'But it's—it's wet.' There was a sharp pause. 'You have got copious quantities of laudanum splashed onto your skirt; why is this?'

She hung her head in shame. 'Because...because I had a bottle of laudanum in my pocket. It smashed when I fell.'

'Oh Anya...' His tone was far more sad than reprimanding.

Sitting on the hard stones with her smarting knees and burning elbows amid the languidly, airlessly slimy red-brown laudanum, Anna felt as though her whole outer facade had smashed too. She felt utterly destitute. Like a snail without its shell. She stared dumbly at the ground.

Without saying a word, Ivanovsky took Anna in his arms. She did not resist. He held her good name in his hands, and to her it felt as though the hands hovered above a bottomless pit.

He lifted her up with ease and carried her towards the back door of the house. She said nothing, and let her head fall limply against his shoulder. Once inside he set her down on a chair in the hall.

'Are you hurt?' he asked gently, kneeling before her.

'My elbows...they got rather the worst of it.'

'May I see?'

She lifted her arms and pushed up her sleeves to expose her elbows. Blood covered them. She flinched and looked away.

He stood up. 'Let me get something for that.'

He returned a short while later with a bowl, a cloth, a roll of bandage and a jar of salve. She remained silent and fixed her eyes on the ceiling while he carefully began cleaning her grazed elbows.

'I do not hurt you?'

It was hurting her. Everything about him hurt her. His presence was to her heart what the sight of food through a shop window was to a starving pauper. It hurt. It hurt so much.

She looked at him. 'It does not hurt.'

He paused and smiled sadly up at her. 'Saying the moon is square does not make it so.'

Anna felt her face colour slightly. She quickly looked away again. Those dark, tenderly drowsy eyes missed nothing. She was afraid of meeting their gaze. He might see into her soul. He might claim her heart as his own and carry it off.

A soft kiss was placed onto her hand. 'Forgive me, little darling, but life hurts. Lying helps nothing.'

Anna swallowed hard. It was time to change the subject. 'Those clothes you are wearing fit you so well it leads me to suspect your luggage was retrieved?'

'*Oui*, suitcase containing my clothes was retrieved, but—' he gave a pained smile— 'the trunk containing all of my painting tools and all artworks I have done in New Zealand appears to have been swallowed by ocean forever.'

'It...it is not lost...' she faltered, cringing with shame.

His face lit up. 'No?'

'No. I have it.'

'But that is wonderful!'

'It is in my room. But...I am ashamed to admit that I...opened it.' She flinched and looked away, waiting for his storm of indignation to rain down on her.

'Something is the matter?' he asked, holding her hands in his as he looked up at her.

She looked down without thinking. 'You...you are not angry with me?'

'Of course not! My dearest Anya, my heart is filled with joy at hearing you found them and saved them from sea. I was about to don black and go into mourning!'

A smile of relief made an uninvited appearance on her lips. 'Oh. I'm glad.'

'My paintings, did you like them?'

'Your landscapes are beautiful, but—but—'

'Yes?'

'That painting of me—I do not think it a good likeness.'

'And why is that?'

She cast her eyes down. 'Because it is too beautiful.'

'Coming from young lady with a little vanity about her, that is quite lofty criticism.'

'It is not that I dislike the portrait, Mr Ivanovsky. It is just that I am afraid that anyone who—who—'

'Go on.'

'Who believes that that is what I really look like would be

bitterly disappointed if they laid eyes on me in the flesh,' she finished uncertainly.

But before he could answer, they were interrupted by a new arrival.

'How're you, how're you?' cried Mr Sleighman as he scuffled down the hall.

Ivanovsky rose and stepped back.

'It is nothing, just a little graze,' Anna replied as dismissively as she was able.

Mr Sleighman was on his knees in a moment, holding the bowl of water and cloth in unsteady hands. He did not wait for a response from her before starting to dab aimlessly at her grazed elbow. Bloodied water was splashed and dripped all over her as the bumbling attentions continued. The stinging pain that shot through her injured elbow made her eyes water, and she had to clamp her mouth tightly in order not to cry out in pain.

'Mr Sleighman,' interrupted Ivanovsky, 'I think that is enough.'

The reverend turned on the Russian like a poked snake. 'I know what is best for my fiancée!' And with that, he returned to the task with renewed vigour.

A whimper of pain escaped Anna.

Ivanovsky took hold of the bowl. 'The lady, she is hurting.'

Mr Sleighman seized the bowl and yanked it off Ivanovsky. The sudden force threw a wave of water all down Anna's front. She gasped with disgust, and Mr Sleighman stared at the accident in shock.

The sheer awfulness of his thick, squashed nose hit her with crippling force. Anna could not bear to look at it for a single second longer. She got hold of the empty bowl, turned it upside down and thrust it over Mr Sleighman's head. After taking a moment to survey the very pleasing result, she swept into the parlour.

'Sorry...' Mr Sleighman's muffled voice trailed after her.

Ivanovsky followed her into the parlour, a roll of bandage, a pair of scissors and a jar of salve in his hands.

She sat down and held her arms out for him. The Russian wore a troubled look as he carefully set about finishing the task in silence, clearly disturbed by the word 'fiancée'.

Anna was careful to avoid looking him in the eyes, as she knew he was wondering how she could marry such a man. His questioning eyes were not welcome, for how could she answer him when she barely knew herself?

A few minutes later, Mr Sleighman knocked softly on the open door and slunk timidly into the room. He loitered near the door, obviously hoping for an apology from her.

Trying to avoid looking at two men at once left only one place to look. The ceiling. Her eyes remained fixed on it.

Mr Sleighman, meet disappointment. And take care you make a friend of him, because you are sure to be seeing a lot of each other. Such was her line of thought as she sat staring at the ceiling.

When Ivanovsky had finished bandaging her up, she rose. 'Thank you, Mr Ivanovsky. You make an excellent nurse.'

He made a slight bow. 'It was a pleasure, Miss Brown. You make excellent patient.'

A huff of disagreement came from the still awkwardly loitering

Mr Sleighman. Anna could not help exchanging a secret smile with Ivanovsky.

Then she swept off up to her bedroom, still smiling a slight smile to herself. With his formal 'Miss Brown', Ivanovsky had dispelled her fears. Her secret was safe with him. He only wanted her to be happy. Because he loved her.

5

No, it is Not You I Love

AS SHE was now clearly up and about, Anna could not easily get out of dinner in the formal dining room that evening. Out of respect for Anna's reportedly fragile state of health, Jennifer had only asked one guest to dine with the family. Mr Sleighman was to be there at eight, and dinner was to be served at half past. Mr Ivanovsky, the maid informed her mistress, was still too tired to come down and would be eating in his room.

Anna sighed at the face looking back at her from the mirror. She wondered what Ivanovsky had been about to say before Mr Sleighman had interrupted. Perhaps she would never know. That would be a pity, because Ivanovsky seemed to have had a ready response. A kind, thoughtful response.

'N, it is almost dinnertime!' came Jennifer's call from outside Anna's bedroom door.

'I will be out in a moment, Jen.'

Anna tugged fretfully at the neckline of her dress. Why could it not be higher? Her décolletage might not have been the most generous, but that did not stop Mr Sleighman constantly staring at it over his soup.

She chose a black velvet ribbon with a brooch at its centre. Hopefully it would bring his gaze up a little higher.

But halfway through tying it on, she suddenly stopped and threw it back onto the table. How foolish, of course it would not work!

With that, she swept out of her room and down the staircase. The formal downstairs rooms were brightly lit, and gay chatter drifted out from the dining room.

A moment after Anna entered, Mr Sleighman was at her side. 'Hello, how're you?' His manner was somewhere between bashful schoolboy and grovelling slave.

'I am quite well, thank you.' Her tone was carefully neutral.

He looked around to confirm that no one else was within earshot. 'I want to apologise for spilling water over you like that. It should not have happened.'

'It is no matter. My anger towards you was not personal. My nerves were in such a state I do not know what I was thinking of!' laughed Anna.

But inside she was screaming. Mr Sleighman never wasted any time before getting busy grovelling when he suspected he was not in favour. And she always dismissed the offence as nothing. She did this because she thought that she must be forgiving, and not hurt his sensitive feelings. Everyone said how nice he was, how sensitive he was, how he must be encouraged to be more confident.

All evening, like a clockwork doll, Anna's head nodded agreement, her gayest party laugh pealed forth and polite, charming nothings gushed from her mouth. Everyone said how well she looked, how she had bloomed already at the prospect of her marriage, how she was in such high spirits.

But inside she was dead and empty. She was pitifully grateful when at last she had miserably giggled her way through Mr Sleighman's clumsy, groping, tipsy goodnight in the entrance hall, and could exit stage right.

The heat in the dining room had been stifling. Anna's cheeks burned with a fevered heat, and her head ached. Holding a near-overflowing glass of wine, she slipped out the parlour's French doors and onto the veranda. Then into the cool, dark garden she passed, drinking in the peaceful presence of the moonlit summer night. When she reached the walled herb garden, she paused. The distant murmur of the waves joined with the soft chirp of grass crickets.

She breathed deeply and sighed. Alone at last. What a relief…

But a rustle among the darkened foliage reached through the night, and with it came a faint scent; the bittersweet scent of men's aftershave.

If Anna had not been so spent, she would have been more alarmed. 'Sasha, is that you?' she called, looking hard at the dark shape that had just moved in the shadows.

The shadow moved closer, materialising into the form of a man.

Anna turned away with a sigh. A skip of something like gladness leapt in her heart, but yet she was too tired to think or feel much. 'I thought you were still feeling indisposed,' was her murmured greeting to the soft footsteps that came up behind.

The scent now hung thick about her, cloyingly heady. Her aching head throbbed in response to it. She felt gloved hands touch her arms, and after hesitating, they closed around her upper arms. A slight pressure brushed against her back, and a roughly bristled cheek touched against her own fevered one. Then a wet tongue probed her face.

Anna screamed and started, spilling all her wineglass' contents on her dress. 'Mr Sleighman, desist this instant!'

She quickly pulled herself free of the violent embrace, but a hand had her wrist in a fierce grip. 'Sasha?' cried Mr Sleighman savagely. '*Sasha?*' His face was contorted with rage.

Her own anger drained away beneath his furious question. 'He sometimes walks here...I am so tired, so silly—I do not know what I was thinking!' she stammered, cringing with the horror of her mistake.

'*Sasha*, is it?' he shouted, louder this time, and dug his fingernails into her flesh.

'It's the twins—so shamelessly informal! They always call him that—frightfully rude, such an awful habit for me to pick up!'

His nails released her screaming flesh, but the grip remained. His eyes had calmed somewhat, but hate still was there. 'And you'd let him approach you like that? Did you pick *that* habit up from the twins too?'

'No—I knew it was you, of course!' she lied, giving a forced laugh. 'Do pardon me, I'm such a silly thing!' she added, doing her best to simper becomingly.

'You can't help being a woman, I suppose.' His eyes were still narrowed with suspicion. But Anna's simpering did seem to be having something of the hoped-for effect, as he finally let go of her smarting wrist.

'What on earth are you doing here anyhow, Mr Sleighman?' The nervously simpering laugh that she ended the question with made Anna feel like strangling herself.

He narrowed his eyes. 'I was wandering here alone...just thinking of my beloved.'

Anna almost retched. 'Ahem, indeed...'

He put his arm around her waist. She fought hard not to recoil.

'I saw the despicable way that Russian looks at you.' Mr Sleighman tightened his hold. 'He stares at you shamelessly, and his familiarity is disgusting. You are an innocent creature who knows nothing, Anna, but the vile, selfish thoughts in his mind don't escape me. You are a child who does not know this, but all foreigners are not decent like well-bred Englishmen. They have depraved urges worthy only of dogs.'

Anna withered beneath the stale wine fumes that breathed over her along with this little sermon. She did not look at Mr Sleighman, and no sound escaped her.

Mr Sleighman had led Anna towards the seat in the herb garden, where he stopped and moved to stand in front of her before linking his arms around his waist. 'Now that you have been enlightened, we can talk of matters suited to lovers.'

Anna said nothing, and hung her head unhappily.

Mr Sleighman began to move his hands over her waist in clumsy, groping motions. 'I can't wait until we are married. We are going to be so happy.'

'No, Mr Sleighman!' she gasped miserably, stepping back and pushing away his hands.

Mr Sleighman took a silent moment, during which he looked to be swallowing his frustration. Then he looked at Anna.

She was shaking slightly. A painful lump constricted her throat. She looked down.

'Sit, Anna. I need to talk to you.'

Keeping her eyes downcast, she meekly did as he ordered.

He sat down beside her, so close that half her skirt was beneath him and his leg touched her own. 'I have noticed that you shy away from my more *physical* displays of affection.'

She cringed into the corner of the seat. She felt as though she could barely breathe.

'This hurts me,' he continued. 'We are going to be man and wife. You should let me touch you.'

'But—but we are not married yet.'

'But we soon will be. I understand that women normally have no desires of a *physical* nature. A woman is an innocent, child-like thing. She doesn't have desires of the flesh. But what you must understand, Anna, is that the man is different. He is worldlier. It is natural for him to have urges which a woman is a stranger to. It is expected that an innocent child like you will be frightened of worldly things, of worldly feelings.'

Anna's throat felt so tight that she could not swallow, and she could hardly draw breath.

'A woman's pleasure lies in nurturing, giving and self-sacrifice. That is her role, to give. It makes her happy.' He turned to look at her. 'Anna, can I ask you to give me something?'

She nodded dumbly, and did not speak for fear she would sob.

'I want to touch you. I have needs. It is your duty to fulfil them. It will make you happy.'

Anna shivered. She utterly despised herself. She despised her body for the unwelcome advances it caused. She wished she was a man. Men were strong and active, women were nice, caring, weak. She was neither nice nor caring, so that left only weak. She wished she could fall down dead right there. But she remained unfortunately alive, and Mr Sleighman looked at her expectantly.

'I don't—want to,' she choked, turning her head away.

He leaned in closer, and the fumes of his breath blasted down on her. 'Are you selfish? Selfishness is a sin, Anna.'

She just sat there as rigid as a stone statue, wearing an expression as unchanging and unseeing as any to be found carved in marble.

'Are you a sinner, Anna?' he demanded again.

Barely able to keep from recoiling, she shook her head.

He nodded in self-satisfaction. 'Good girl, Anna. Now you know that a woman's body belongs to her husband. I will make an obedient wife of you. A wife that is obedient to her husband is obedient to God, because a husband is head of his household just as Jesus is head of his church.'

Then he started to fumble at the buttons of her dress. But his hands were even more clumsy than usual with feverish excitement.

He made little progress. After only a few attempts, he took hold of the dress and ripped it open.

The tiny fabric-covered buttons burst off in every direction. Some hit Anna's face, and one hit her square in the eye. Water welled in her smarting eye and rolled down her cheek.

With her red corset now plainly displayed, Mr Sleighman became even more fevered. His hands shook, and his wine-reeking breaths came hot and fast on her face. He fumbled uselessly with the laces, which quickly became a hopelessly knotted mess.

He gave the laces an angry jerk. 'Get it open!' He pulled furiously at her corset in an attempt to rip it open. 'Open!'

The whalebones sewn into the corset dug painfully into Anna's ribs as the garment was contorted. 'Mr Sleighman, get your hands off me!' She pushed him roughly back and leapt up. 'Don't think you will be getting everything your way when we are man and wife. My father knows everyone of any consequence in this wretched little colony, and if I wish it, he can make your life very difficult! And I assure you that I intend us to be both equally miserable together, rather than it being I who must carry its full burden while you act like a fool and lord it over me!'

He crumpled. 'Sorry, Anna, I shouldn't have let my love for you overflow like that...'

She regarded him with open contempt. 'You are beneath me, Mr Sleighman. Always remember that.'

Then she hurried for the house.

By the time she reached the back door, she was desperately agitated. She flung the door open and burst in, rushing for the laundry without even pausing to shut the door behind her. The small room was flooded with pale moonlight. By its comfortingly faint silvery light, she tore the soiled silk evening gown off and threw it on the floor. As she did this, Anna gasped and cringed like one who has had the vilest filth thrown over them.

Something metal resting on the windowsill glinted in the moonlight. She slowly reached out towards it. Then she took the small fruit knife in her hand and looked intently down at it. Her own contorted reflection shimmered on the glinting steel blade. She studied it carefully, turning the blade this way and that.

Loathing gripped her. She despised weakness above all things. Mr Sleighman was weak-minded and weak-willed. But still he had made her submit to his will. That made her weaker even than he. The thing that at that moment Anna hated above all things looked up from the coldly glinting blade.

Self-loathing filled her, but, with a gasp, she cast the blade onto the floor and sprung away. Up the stairs and along the hallway Anna sped.

Once in her room, she made straight for the top drawer of the dressing table. She took out a brown glass bottle and carried it over to the bed. There, she threw herself down and snuffed out the lone candle. The only light that pierced the room's heavy gloom was a shaft of ghostly moonlight falling through the open window. A morepork's cry floated on the night air and somewhere in the distance, a dog howled at the moon.

Anna pulled the stopper out of the bottle's neck, put its cold rim to her lips and drained the intensely bitter contents in one gulp.

Then she fell limply back against the pillows and the bottle fell to the floor.

The luridly seductive angel contained within the bottle bore her aloft on its poisonous wings. Out of its mouth breathed enchanting hallucinations that swirled dizzyingly about her in misty rivers. Velvet, inky-black wings brushed against her skin and stupefying waves of ecstasy slowly, languidly oozed through her body. Poisonously lurid colours drifted and sparkled everywhere around.

'Forget, oh forget earthly pains…' whispered the beautiful angel with the dark blue skin, gazing straight at her with hypnotic deep purple eyes.

Anna abandoned herself completely to the dusky angel's pleasures. She gorged herself on the lurid sensations that lived within the strangely glowing purple eyes, and within minutes she could not even remember what pain was.

But as she returned from the pit of poisonous pleasures, strange horrors approached. The dusky angel leaned low over her neck. Suddenly, its silver teeth were embedded in her flesh as it feasted on her blood.

She tried to open her mouth to scream, but clay-like fingers pressed tightly over her lips. The feathered inky-velvet wings closed around her in a stifling embrace. The dark angel threw its head back and, with her warm blood running down its face, groaned aloud with ecstasy.

6

The Snowdrifts Melt

ALMOST midday. Anna yawned wearily and groped for the hand mirror lying on the bedside table. After pulling herself up to lean back against the headboard, she held the mirror up. A pale, gaunt face stared back at her with hollow, blood-shot eyes underlined by dark circles. She groaned and flung the brutal mirror down.

A knock sounded on the door. 'N, you have not forgotten about the tennis party, I hope?'

Anna rolled onto her side and snuggled back into the warm bedclothes. 'Go away.'

The door opened. 'Enough of this slothfulness. Get up and get dressed! The guests will be here shortly.'

Anna groaned again. She *had* forgotten about the tennis party. She hated tennis.

She pulled the bedclothes over her head. 'I am wretchedly tired.'

'What rot. You mope about all day doing nothing.' Jennifer pulled the curtains open with loud screeches that made Anna wince. 'Mrs Dean and the Miss Deans are coming over, and of course also Mr Sleighman.'

'The amount of time Mr Sleighman spends here at Gravemore is so great that he really ought to simply move in. It would save him that tiresome fifteen-minute walk.'

'N, I do not care for that tone. Poor Mr Sleighman does not deserve such unkindness. Any other bride-to-be would be delighted to have such regular proofs of her future husband's love and devotion. Now, I am sending up Molly to help you dress. You will be down in your best summer dress in half an hour: is that clear?'

'Yes...'

Half an hour later, Anna swept out onto the veranda dressed in a light cotton gown of pale mint green sprigged with a print of purple cherries and red strawberries. A little straw hat trimmed with white lace and red polka-dot ribbon was perched on her swept-up brown hair, and cotton net gloves of pale cream completed the picture.

She had only just made her entrance when a frilly-capped head poked around the corner of the door. 'Sorry to bother you, Miss Anna, but what do you want me to do with that evening gown lying on the washhouse floor?'

Anna turned calmly to Molly. 'I want you to burn it.'

The maid's eyebrows shot up in surprise. 'Burn it?'

'Yes, burn it,' Anna repeated stonily.

Looking a little disturbed, Molly bobbed. 'Right you are, Miss Anna!'

When the housemaid's light, hurrying footsteps had receded in the direction of the laundry, Anna turned her attention to the scene before her.

On the turf tennis court in front of the veranda, the game was already in progress. The three white-frocked Miss Deans were engaged in a vigorous game of doubles. Mr Sleighman, who appeared to be having some difficulty keeping up with the furious speed of the young Dean girls, made up the numbers.

The loud, brash chorus of dozens of lazily chirping cicadas filled the hot, still air. Just watching the enthusiastic sport played out under the beating sun made Anna feel hot and tired. She sunk into one of the cane chairs sitting on the veranda.

After only a few minutes, footsteps approached from inside. She would know that tread anywhere. It was Ivanovsky's. She tensed.

A moment later, he was standing before her holding out a tray containing tall glasses of lemonade and a plate of Turkish delight. 'Drink?'

She smiled a faint, guarded smile and took one of the cool glasses. 'Thank you.'

The informality of Ivanovsky's dress shocked her. He wore a white shirt, the sleeves rolled up almost to the elbow, a red and blue paisley silk waistcoat, completely unbuttoned, and a horrifically casual blue silk necktie knotted in a voluminous bow. At least Mr Sleighman did not turn up at parties half-dressed.

He set the tray down on a low table and chose the chair opposite her own.

Anna suddenly became aware that Ivanovsky was quietly

laughing. At her, it seemed. She frowned crossly. 'What?'

'Even at little outdoor gathering in the heat of summer, in remote part of remote little colony, you English tut-tut about a gentleman taking his jacket off.' He laughed softly, shaking his head.

Anna turned her head away sulkily. 'Is that all Russians turn up for; to laugh at us English?'

'You had a bad trip?' The warm, low voice was now deadly serious.

She kept her head turned. 'What nonsense you talk. I have been nowhere.'

'Not your body. But during the night your mind has, I think, traversed a great many miles in the enthralling embrace of your beloved opium angel.'

Anna's heart jumped with shock, but there was clearly no point trying to deny it. She took a miserable sip of lemonade and stared down at her hands. 'Are all Russians mind readers as well as slovenly dressers?'

'I had friend in St Petersburg who was opium eater. Your enslavement is written in your face.'

Without meaning to, she looked up. 'What...what happened to him?'

'He became ever more enamoured with opium, until day came when he did nothing but lie about stupefied. Then one morning I come to his apartment and...he is cold and dead.' Ivanovsky gazed sadly into the distance. 'Yuri was talented poet and kind-hearted man. It was such waste...such terrible waste...'

'I am sorry for your loss.'

His eyes suddenly fixed on hers. 'Anya, do not throw away the life that has been given to you.'

She looked him squarely in the eye for the first time since the ball. 'What if I hate the life that has been given to me?'

'You hate the iron straightjacket of convention you insist on forcing yourself into every day.'

She turned away angrily. 'You know nothing of my life!'

'I know everything about your life, little darling. It is written in your sad grey eyes,' came the gentle reply.

She coldly, calmly looked at him again. 'This is how I have chosen to live my life. Wild behaviour and irresponsibility are not for me. I have chosen to be a dutiful and obedient daughter and good Christian rather than pursue my own selfish desires.'

He smiled sadly. 'Anya, you have not chosen this life. You are merely too afraid to live any other life.'

She stiffened. 'Are you calling me a coward?'

'Yes.' Laughing his soft, deep laugh, he held out his hand. 'Here, you can slap me if you feel insulted.'

This unexpected response defused her anger, and she could not help smiling slightly. 'I do not care about your crack-pot ideas. Artists are not in the least bit sane.'

'If thinking differently from rest of society is conclusive sign of mental derangement, then I am guilty.'

'Sasha, Sasha!' came eleven-year-old Miss Mabel and Miss Mandy's cries as they raced for the veranda, while their fifteen-year-old sister Millie walked beside Mr Sleighman some way behind, with her hand under his arm.

This ended Anna's involuntary heart-to-heart, and a moment later Ivanovsky had one young Dean twin hanging around his shoulders while the other sat in his lap.

Anna cocked a surprised eyebrow. Ivanovsky clearly had been up and about more than she had realised.

The two freckled, strawberry-blonde girls chattered loudly and excitedly. 'We only won by one point!' cried Mabel.

'Yes,' shrieked an indignant Mandy, 'Mr Sleighman cheated!'

'Mother was meant to be empire, but she went wandering off looking at some flower or other instead!'

'And Millie lied and said he hadn't cheated!'

'Yeah, silly Millie is utterly crushed on Mr Sleighman!'

'And—and he said he didn't!'

'But he is such a hornswoggler!'

'Totally, just so; a total cheat!'

Ivanovsky was shaking with laughter by now. 'Mabya, Manduska, don't both talk at once or I shall become deaf as old man!'

Mabel ruffled his hair in a manner Anna thought shockingly impolite. 'Well, your hair *is* already the right colour!'

'Yeah, are all Russians born with grey hair?' demanded Mandy, giving the silver mane a tug.

He tickled Mabel under the arms.

'Oh, stop, stop, stop!' shrieked the laughing girl, now pulling at his hands rather than his hair.

'Are all Russians born with grey hair?' Mandy asked again, more loudly this time.

'No, *printseca*, they are not,' he replied good-humouredly.

Anna's eyebrows reached even greater heights. Not only had the girls already received that most Russian of things, a diminutive form of their names, but they were being called what she presumed were Russian pet names too. The Dean twins did not diddle about.

'What's wrong with you then?' asked Mandy.

'Yeah,' Mabel chipped in, 'was one of your ancestors a polar bear?'

Ivanovsky laughed so hard that Mabel nearly fell out of his lap. The two girls shrieked with laughter, and even Anna allowed herself a little smile at all the merriment. But Millie Dean just turned her pretty little nose up at such childishness and continued flirting with Mr Sleighman down at the far end of the veranda.

'I was not born with grey hair,' the Russian said when he had stopped laughing enough to speak. 'When I was boy I had dark hair, but it start going grey when I was not much older than your big sister.'

'I hope *you* were never as silly as *that*,' said Mandy, rolling her eyes at the giggling Millie, who stood close beside Mr Sleighman as they both leaned on the rail.

'I am too much of a gentleman to answer such delicate question.'

A moment later, the three of them were sprawled on the deck in a helplessly laughing heap as the chair collapsed. Anna very much suspected Mandy had something to do with the chair's failure.

'Children, whatever are you doing?' screamed Mrs Dean as she hurtled up to the veranda. 'Shameless, shameless girls!'

The laughing heap made some half-hearted efforts to disentangle.

'Mr Ivanovsky, I sincerely apologise for my daughters' terrible behaviour,' gasped Mrs Dean, surveying the sight before her in horror. 'All that time they spend loitering about with the farmhands and reading vulgar novels; it has quite ruined them!'

Ivanovsky at last broke free. Anna very much suspected some effort had gone into trying to keep him pinned down.

'My dear lady, it is I who must apologise. I am afraid I rather encourage them,' he said, still smiling broadly.

The handsome Russian's charm proved very effective oil to Mrs Dean's troubled waters. She coloured like a young girl. 'Well, there is no harm done, I suppose.'

Millie and Mr Sleighman soon joined the rest of the group around the refreshment tray. Mr Sleighman looked peeved. Anna knew why. He had been hoping she would notice young Millie Dean's flirtations and become jealous. That Ivanovsky had been the centre of everyone's attention instead had greatly hurt his feelings. Anna knew Mr Sleighman had been doing it in revenge for the incident in the hallway the other day. She did not care for such pettiness, and she did not care if Mr Sleighman flirted.

Jennifer bustled out with a tray of iced tea and little shortcake rounds topped with clotted cream and diced strawberries. 'Do help yourselves, everyone.'

Mabel and Mandy led the charge, and soon the tray's contents were held in sticky hands or piled onto dainty china.

Jennifer turned to Anna. 'You are looking frightfully pale. A nice game of tennis will bring a little colour back. Perhaps you might like to partner Mr Sleighman?'

Anna put her strawberry shortcake back onto her plate. 'But Jen, you know I detest tennis!'

'What has got into you lately? You are such a misery.'

Mr Sleighman drew in cajolingly close. 'Come on, it will be great.'

Jennifer smiled at Mr Sleighman. 'Anna, you absolutely cannot disappoint your poor fiancé. You must play. I insist.'

Anna sighed. 'Very well...'

'Do you play, Mr Ivanovsky?' asked Jennifer.

He shook his head. 'I do not. I spend such large amount of time hauling easels up mountains and over moors that I have no wish for yet more running about.'

'Oh dear, what a pity. I daresay Mrs Dean and I shall have to oppose your team in that case, Anna.'

Anna looked at the half-empty glass of iced tea she held. 'Might I be permitted to finish my tea before being mustered onto the field?'

'Oh certainly. But do not go wandering off anywhere.'

Anna's lips tightened in annoyance. Her sister was beginning to sound just like Mother. Being married did not give one the right to suddenly start ordering about unmarried sisters. She swept off in search of company that was more agreeable.

Mabel and Mandy sat on a bench a little apart from the others, busily feeding an unbroken line of strawberry shortcake and Turkish delight into their mouths. There were always plenty of larks with the Dean twins.

Anna smiled and sat down beside them. 'So, how come you two are already so well acquainted with Mr Ivanovsky?'

Mabel paused the continuous chain mid-shortcake. 'Oh, we have been riding over every afternoon to visit him.'

Then Mandy's Turkish delight paused briefly. 'Yeah, invalids must be kept amused.'

'Why did you never go in to see him, Anna?' Mabel's question seemed a little accusing in tone.

'Well, because I—I felt it would be improper for a young lady to visit a gentleman in his bedroom.'

'Oh what, scared you might see him wearing only his shirt and faint?'

'Yeah, prissy missy!'

Anna flinched. But she was more interested in talk about the Russian guest than she cared to admit, so pushed down her heated retort.

She swallowed hard. 'No, I merely did not wish to make Mr Ivanovsky feel uncomfortable by forcing him to receive a lady in such an informal setting.'

'Sasha does not care about such things.'

'Yeah, he lets us do anything.'

'He is such a lark!'

'Totally, just so.'

'You already act like an old maid of a hundred and two, Anna.'

'Yeah, you are vastly buttoned down.'

Anna nearly choked on her tea. 'Mabel, you must not say such things! It is quite impolite.'

'Even if it's true?' piped Mandy.

Anna set her tea down firmly. 'How dare you!'

The twins just giggled.

Anna rose and swept off in a huff. Horrible brats.

Whispers of 'prissy missy' and 'vastly frosty' followed her retreat.

By now, all of the players in the next match were ready. Mr Sleighman handed Anna a racquet, then escorted her to the court with his arm around her waist.

Out of the corner of her eye, she caught Mabel and Mandy giggling at the stiffly cringing look she obviously had about her. Those two really did need a good clout about the ears. She was tempted to stick her tongue out at them.

But she did not. She was not about to let a pair of graceless brats goad her into impoliteness. Anna lifted her head high. She was above such things.

Although Anna would not admit it to anyone, including herself, the chief reason why she hated tennis was because she was terrible at it. She could not bear to make a fool of herself in public. She missed every single tennis ball that came her way. A game which involved running about in the most appallingly unladylike manner whilst madly swatting at thin air like a lunatic was not her idea of fun. It was her idea of hell.

She almost felt as though the eyes of the watching Ivanovsky and Dean girls were boring a hole in her head. After only a short while, Anna began to feel unbearably hot and wretched.

As Mr Sleighman trudged to receive yet another of her missed balls, she turned to Jennifer. 'I really am feeling quite unwell. This heat is simply awful!'

Jennifer came up to the net. 'N, stop being such a moaner. I have had enough of this rot. Now get back over there and play properly for once!'

Anna felt five years old. Wretched weariness sat heavily upon her, and beads of sweat stung at her eyes. The ball came hurtling towards her. She ducked.

'N, stop fooling around!'

'You know I cannot play very well!'

'Perhaps,' said Mr Sleighman, 'I could give you a few tips?'

'Very well,' said Jennifer. 'You show Anna how to play properly, and Mrs Dean and I will have a little rest.'

'Now, you hold the racquet like this,' the delighted Mr Sleighman instructed her. 'And for the backhand stroke, you move like so...' He pressed his front tightly against her back and moved her arm into the required position.

His hot, garlic-scented breath blasted her already boiling neck, and his sticky sweat soaked all the way through the back of her dress. She had never felt more unladylike.

'I really think I need to sit down—'

'And then you move your hand forwards...' As he moved her arm forwards, he thrust his pelvis against the voluminous bustle of her dress.

She gasped. 'Oh Mr Sleighman, I really do need a rest—'

There was another thrust. 'Just follow that stroke through...'

She felt like a boiling bag pudding. 'I'm starting to see stars!'

His sharp chin was resting on her neck. 'Good, just how it should be...'

'No—I—I...' Then the world went dark around her and she started to fall. She was dimly aware of hitting the turf with a thud.

* * * *

Ivanovsky's concerned face swam before her eyes. 'Miss Brown, are you well?' He shook her gently. 'Miss Anna?'

She became vaguely aware that she was lying on the grass, and that the sound of tense voices were all around. 'I...I...feel faint,' she managed to whisper.

'Shall I carry you inside?'

She nodded weakly.

'Perhaps up to your room, so you can loosen your corset?'

Although she was ever so proud of her twenty-two-inch waist, there could be negative sides to such tight lacing. Anna felt as though she could barely breathe. 'Yes...'

'Out of the way!' The voice was Mr Sleighman's. 'I'm handling this. She's going to be my wife, not yours!' He then pushed aside Ivanovsky in the most ungentlemanly manner.

The Russian backed away without protest.

Anna could now see clearly again, but her legs still felt like badly set jelly. Mr Sleighman put his arms around her and heaved. He barely made it to his feet. Then he began the slow, wobbling journey towards the door.

Anna whimpered with fear, as at every step she seemed about to be dropped. The door was painfully reached, then the parlour was crossed. Sweat was pouring off Mr Sleighman in rivers by this stage. Mr Ivanovsky stood well back. But everyone else crowded around. It was so humiliating. She wished they would all just go away—perhaps to locate a zoo which was wanting an elephant. No more food for a week. That golden twenty-one inches must be reached. Even if it killed her.

Mr Sleighman reached the bottom of the stairs. The rug there was uneven. Mr Sleighman's little foot made contact with the rug. Everyone gasped. Then they stood staring silently at the wreckage.

'Sorry...'

Anna pulled her head up off the floor. Mercifully, Ivanovsky was nowhere to be seen. Such tact.

Mr Sleighman had his arms back around her in a flash. He heaved. She barely cleared the ground. He adjusted his grip. He heaved again. Still no luck.

Anna was almost crying now. The humiliation was worse than any nightmare she had ever had. She truly wished she was dead. 'Enough!' she screamed suddenly.

Everyone fell into a hushed awe. Except Mr Sleighman. He was still trying to lift her.

She struck him across the face. He wordlessly stepped back, nursing his red cheek. She then began slowly crawling up the stairs on her hands and knees. Mr Sleighman made as if to move towards her.

'No!' she screamed over her shoulder.

She ascended step by painful step. No one dared move. Once up the stairs, she pulled herself to her feet with the aid of the hall table and staggered along to her door, hands against the wall for support.

She opened the door, entered and slammed it shut. Then she

locked it. Now it was safe. She flung herself facedown onto the bed and buried her head in a pillow. Then she finally allowed the tears to flow. Unending rivers poured forth, and howls of agony accompanied the river of tears.

A knock sounded on the door a few moments later. 'N, are you all right?'

'What a stupid question! If I were all right, I would not be like this, would I?' Anna picked up the empty glass bottle still lying on the floor and was about to throw it at the door. Then she changed her mind and let it fall again.

What was the point? Besides, it might damage the paintwork. She just settled for a fresh flood of tears instead.

'N, open the door!'

'Go away!'

'Open it at once!'

After a long pause, Jennifer at last gave up and Anna heard her footsteps retreating back down the hallway.

Some while later, a very cautious little knock sounded on the door. 'I want to apologise for dropping you like that... I should've seen that uneven mat...'

Anna put a pillow over her head and just cringed with excruciating embarrassment. Even an elephant would likely think she was too big. She hated herself.

'Anna, I'm sorry...'

Why would he not just go away and die?

'Anna, say something...'

'I hate you!'

'That's not very nice...' came his hurt, whining voice.

'I hate you, I hate you, I hate you!'

The soft pad of Mr Sleighman scuffling back down the hallway reached her ears. She breathed a sigh of relief and got back to the business of crying.

No one else disturbed her silent misery until six that evening, when there was a gentle tap on her door. 'Anna, it's Mabel.'

'And Mandy.'

'We thought you might be hungry.'

'Yeah, we'd starve to death if we went this long without food.'

'So we've brought a tray up.'

'Just so. There's cold tongue, salad with mayonnaise, and trifle—'

'With lots and lots of custard—'

'And jelly—'

'With lots and lots of cream on top.'

'Totally, just so.'

'If we leave it on the floor outside your door, will you come and get it?'

Anna sat on her bed listening. Perhaps they were not so horrid after all. 'Yes, that is very kind of you two,' she croaked

'And we are sorry about what we said earlier.'

'Yeah, it was mean to poke you up like that.'

'Totally, just so.'

'That Mr Sleighman is an utter hugger-mugger.'

'Yeah, utterly sly. Look at the way he was making eyes at silly Millie.'

'Slimy gal-sneaker. And he's nowhere near as good at tennis as he claims.'

'Cheater.'

'Just so. He's such a foozler.'

'Total bungler. Being put into an all-round muddle by him doesn't make you a prissy missy.'

'But she is vastly buttoned up about Sasha though,' came Mandy's tactless aside to her twin.

'Yeah, that's because she's in love with him, dopey.'

'A pity he's not afternoonified enough for her, chuckaboo.'

Anna's jaw was down near the ground. These rural children really were utterly shameless.

'And you saw the way Sasha was looking at her. He thinks she's bang up to the elephant.'

'Yeah, I'm never going to hang up my ladle for a man unless he looks at me like that.'

'Totally so. Me neither.'

'It was vastly adorable.'

'Don't know what he sees in her, though.' Their voices were starting to fade down the hall.

'She looks like a good sandwich would kill her.'

'And she's vastly buttoned up...'

'Yeah, she's a total misery guts; always seems to have the morbs...'

'Don't know why she bothers pretending otherwise...'

'She is well silly choosing that hornswoggling meater over Sasha...'

And then their voices could be heard no more.

Anna was particularly thoughtful as she munched her way through the generous piles of food. The twins were absolutely shameless. Their *language.* Hornswoggler for cheat, meater for coward, foozler for bungler; it almost made her eyes water. And they were *unspeakably* rude. Then again...maybe they had a point. But her in love with Ivanovsky? No, love was not for her. Love was for the likes of Miss Dora. For wild romantics determined to shame their family and ruin their life.

She chewed determinedly on a large mouthful of cold tongue. Soon the wool boat would be visiting. Soon Sasha Ivanovsky would sail out of her life forever and she would be a married woman.

Perhaps she did love him. Men like him were always dangerous to weak feminine hearts. But in the end, it really did not matter. She was going to live a life which society would approve of, and that was that.

But as Anna lay there in the gathering dusk with only a ticking clock for company, uncomfortable fears pressed themselves close. What would her wedding night be like?

As the darkness crept further and further into her room, the thoughts became ever more uncomfortable. She knew she would have to face Mr Sleighman's assault without the help of the dusky angel's stupefying embrace. That had been the one thing that made the thought of his body, his hands, all over her bearable. And it was the one thing that erased Ivanovsky from her mind. But she was too afraid to ask the doctor for another bottle. He would not believe her story of the accident on the patio, and would think she had drunk it all in a matter of days. That might bring him to approach Mr

Sleighman or Jennifer with concerns about her. No, she could not ask for another bottle.

She was desperate for opium. It would fade out the distasteful visions and sickening sensations that flitted all around her as she thought of sharing Mr Sleighman's bed. It would fade out the longing, the desperate, desperate longing to surrender to her heart once. Just once. She tossed and turned sleeplessly for a good while.

At last she could bear it no longer. She got up and went over to the shelf the cheerfully smiling Russian doll set on.

7

Oh, Sweet Night

Taking the Russian doll in her hands, Anna looked down at it. One night of love. Just one night of love to cherish in her memory. Just one night of love to hold close through all the nights of misery. Surely she could face this life if she had that?

Anna glided silently to the door, turned the key and exited the room.

From under the door next to her own, a faint light shone forth. Good, he was still awake.

Her heart pounded uncomfortably as she softly knocked.

'Yes?' came his heavenly voice from within.

'It's—it's Anna. Might I come in?'

'Of course you may, darling.'

She entered and quietly closed the door behind her.

Shirtless, he was sitting up in bed holding a book and a pair of reading glasses he appeared to have just removed.

Anna faltered uncertainly. Modesty demanded she lower her eyes, but she could not. Even if she had gazed upon Ivanovsky for a hundred years, Anna felt she would be loathe to look away.

He smiled at her. 'I look like a book-wormish old professor wearing these, but too many dark Russian winters spent squinting at books whilst burning only one candle for economy, they have done for me.'

Anna nervously returned his smile. She did not believe he could look like an old professor, book-wormish or otherwise. The smooth skin of his naked upper body was bathed in the soft golden light cast by the lone candle resting on the bedside table. His broad shoulders, muscular upper arms and sculpted chest were the very essence of strong, virile manhood. No, for all his wise thoughtfulness, there was nothing old or decrepit about Sasha Ivanovsky.

Still smiling a pleased and welcoming smile, he lay back against the pillows like Poseidon against the foaming ocean waves. 'Excuse my state of undress, but nights here are terribly hot for a Russian bear.'

She realised she must have been staring. But Mabel and Mandy had been wrong. Anna had not fainted. Her mind had just gone blank instead.

Ivanovsky patted the space on the edge of the bed. 'Come, sit and tell me.'

She crept up to him. 'Are you sure you will not be squashed?'

'Little Anya, you could not squash me if you tried.'

He was right. Nervously and carefully, she sat down. 'I—I hope I am not disturbing you. I could not sleep and...'

'Not at all, I am delighted to see you. I was afraid for you after Mr Sleighman's foolishness earlier at the tennis party. Humiliating lady in such manner is unkind.'

She nodded. 'I assure you that I was not hurt in the accident.'

'Yes you were. Your feelings were terribly wounded. He made you feel like lumbering elephant.'

Her head lifted with a start. 'How did you know?'

'Because your face was inscribed with humiliation, and because your corset you still are wearing underneath that dressing robe.'

She gave a defeated nod. 'You miss nothing.'

'I am sorry.'

She silently brought the hand holding the Russian doll out from amongst the folds of her silk robe.

'Ah, you found it. Often I wonder about that.'

She felt her cheeks warm slightly. 'Yes, I did...'

She was silent for a few moments, hoping he would say something. But he just patiently waited, his loving dark eyes resting peacefully on her.

Fidgeting with the folds of the bed sheet, she swallowed hard. 'That day in the park...' But her courage faltered and she fell silent once more.

He placed a warm hand gently over hers. 'Ask me anything.'

'That day in the park you said that—that you loved me—' She looked up. 'But I do not really know what true love is—I doubt that there is such a thing at all!'

He smiled his languid, melting smile. There seemed to her to be more secrecy in it than usual. 'Indeed.'

She almost felt annoyed that he did not react to this. Any other enamoured lover would have leapt to the defence.

'Go on, dear one.'

'My family would say they love me. However, I believe that they merely love what they see of themselves in me, and that they feel duty-bound to love me. Mr Sleighman believes that the feelings he bears towards me are those of ardent love. But I believe it is merely carnal lust mistaken for something deeper.'

'I think you are right.'

'But—but...'.'

He gently squeezed her hand. 'I am listening.'

'You told me that you love me. I do not believe you.' She boldly watched for the effect of her provocative words.

His smile only deepened. Lines of laughter danced around his heavy-lidded eyes as he thoughtfully tilted his head to one side.

She gave a piqued toss of the head. 'Well?'

'I do believe, Miss Anya, that you wish me to convince you.'

'Yes. Convince me that love really exists.'

'I will not try to convince you of any such thing,' he answered slowly, 'but I will tell you what I mean when I say that I love you.'

She nodded, her attention completely fixed on him.

'There is special place in my heart reserved just for you. It is always there; you are free to come and go from it as you please. I have no wish to lock your spirit in like caged songbird or fetter you to me like slave. My love will always allow you to be free. If you choose to be at my side, I will bestow every kindness, help and comfort that it is in my power to give to you. In return, I ask for nothing. That is what I mean when I say that I love you.'

'Nothing?'

'Nothing. I desire only your wellbeing.'

She gazed at him in solemn silence. There could be no doubting his love. It was true, pure, unselfish.

'Why do you love me?' she asked at last. 'Mabel and Mandy tell me I am mean, miserable and boring. What is there to love about me?'

He laughed gently. 'They are right in some ways. However, within every dull cocoon is a beautiful butterfly. Your butterfly, Anya, is spectacularly beautiful. But you must let it go free so that it can be warmed by the sunlight and take flight.'

She shook her head sadly. 'A life of such beautiful poetry is not for earth-dwellers like me.'

He gave her hand a rebuking squeeze. 'I heed you not. One day you will break free of your dark, earth-bound prison and spread gilded, shimmering wings as you rise up towards the sun. I know you will, because I believe in you.'

Anna shook her head again, but said no more. She held the brightly painted Russian doll out to him. 'This little doll has given me comfort in the dark, lonely hours of the night, but she cannot accompany me any further on my journey. When I enter my husband's home as a bride she must not come with me. Tokens of love from past sweethearts have no place in a wife's home.'

Sadness filled his eyes as he reluctantly took it. 'Oh Anya, why do you torment yourself?'

Ignoring this, she continued. 'Thank you for the notes. They are beautiful. I came to treasure them.'

'I am glad.'

Then she paused uncertainly, overcome with shyness. 'There—there is something I long to have in place of this doll...'

'What is it?'

She felt her cheeks grow hot once more. 'I—I—do not know how to say this...'

He put his hand to her cheek. 'Do not blush so, little one. You can ask me for anything.'

She bit her lip reluctantly and looked down, a furious blush spreading over her face.

His bemused puzzlement deepened. 'What is it? Anya, you can tell me.'

'Have—have you ever—lain with a woman?'

A teasing spark lighted in his eyes. 'Ah, now I understand. The answer to your question, mademoiselle, is yes. I was married briefly as young man. But my wife and I, we were very young and after a few years we found our paths had wandered far from each others. Our divorce, it was amicable.'

'Oh.' Anna was rather shocked. She did not know anyone who was divorced, and the casualness with which he talked about it was almost more shocking to her than the divorce itself.

'Is that all?' he asked slowly.

'No...I...I...' She felt the familiar tightness starting to close around her throat. 'I—am so—so afraid of—of—'

'Of your wedding night?' he suggested gently.

She nodded and kept her eyes down, much too embarrassed to look at him. 'Yes. I—I—I cannot bear the thought of—of *him* touching me,' she choked, barely able to say the words.

'And?'

'And I want, just once, to feel...' Her words trailed off as her courage failed her.

He squeezed her hand gently. 'Go on.'

'Oh Sasha, I want to feel what it is to lay in your arms and be utterly yours! To quench the thirst, the torment—' Anna suddenly fell silent.

Rhapsody had been breathed across his face by her words, and its thrall was dangerous. A silent voice screamed out at the folly and risk of what she doing. 'I—I—' she stammered desperately.

'Anya, there is no need.' His eyes seemed darker than they ever had as he reached his hand out to her. 'You have so many words when your eyes, they have said everything already.'

Anna dared to look up again. 'Will—will you make love to me?' She whispered it quietly, as if afraid the very walls might think her words disgraceful.

'You are sure?'

She nodded shyly, still hanging her head.

'You will not be tormented with regret at breaking rules of propriety and disobeying laws of your religion?'

She shook her head. It did not matter what you did as long as no one knew about it. 'Please, let me have this one thing. I could bear anything if I had that memory to cherish!'

Conflict clouded his face. 'Society's rules are as nothing, but dishonour is not. You have promised yourself to another.'

'Please...'

After a moment's silence, he finally nodded. 'One night. But there is one condition, little darling.'

'What is that?' she whispered.

'You must kiss me first.'

She looked up nervously. 'Me?'

The heavy-lidded eyes were dancing with teasing laughter. 'Yes, you.' He then lay back on the pillows and closed his eyes.

She just stared down at the silver-maned Adonis. He clearly wished there to be no doubts about who had initiated this. This was a perfectly fair stance. Unfortunately, she did not even know where, or indeed how, to begin. To do such a bold and shameless thing, to be so forward and daring—it was not proper.

He slightly opened his eyes for a moment. 'Still I wait...'

She slowly, falteringly leaned down over him. But the face peacefully glowing in the candlelight had such an air of quiet majesty that it caused her to pause in awe.

Contained within that face seemed to be the very soul of Russia. Her dusky forests, her broad steppes, her snow covered fields glinting beneath pale starlight, her clear, deep lakes, they were all there. Enwrapping all of this was a peacefulness that seemed rooted in the earth's eternal rhythms. It was a place for the bold. Any woman venturing in might never find her way out. But Anna knew she could not live without doing what she longed to.

Taking a slow breath, she stooped once more. His lips, brimming with sensitivity and tender emotion, were slightly parted. As her hesitant lips lightly touched down on his, she felt like a traveller who, having trudged many long, dusty miles over endless barren plains, at last stoops to drink from cool, brimming waters. She softly, softly kissed his warm, yielding lips.

She then slowly let out the breath she had been holding. 'Was—was that satisfactory?'

The gaze of the heavy-lidded eyes rested on her caressingly. 'Like butterfly alighting on petal.' His low response slid over her like thick honey.

She gave a shy but pleased smile.

He reached out and was about to start unfastening her corset, but she stilled his fingers with a hesitant hand. 'I—I—do not like to be seen without this on...'

'Anya, I refuse to make love to you while you are wearing that thing,' he replied good-humouredly but plainly.

Her face puckered in extreme reluctance. 'But I look so fat if I am not wearing a corset...' she whimpered. 'The ideal waist is twenty-one inches. I am a whole inch bigger than that.'

His gentle smile was sympathetic but unrelenting. 'My sweet, your waist, it is tiny. If you were any thinner I would need to wear my glasses or I would not see you at all!'

Her lips could not help breaking into a little smile. However, it was only a moment before another dark cloud blotted out the sun yet again as a second horror presented itself. 'My bosom is pathetic. I have...' She paused to gather courage. 'I have two—' She swallowed hard. 'Two pillow cases stuffed down...there.'

To her surprise, he just laughed softly and shook his head. 'I do not care if you have pillow itself down there as well.'

'Truly?'

'Truly.'

She nodded. He must think her so silly. Filled with such petty concerns. So distastefully ashamed.

His finger was tilting her chin up an instant later. 'No Anya, I am not thinking any of the things you fear I am. Do not convict me of such unkindness.'

She squirmed slightly, as his firm fingers were forcing her to look him in the eyes. She did not want to look him in the eyes. 'I'm sorry...' she murmured uncomfortably.

His somewhat stern expression softened. 'Just stop thinking, Anya. You poke and pinch your every urge and feeling with that sharp little mind until they are either dead or huddled in corner quaking with fear.'

She knew he was right. Nevertheless, she did not wish to admit it. So she merely gave a pained little smile instead.

The look he gave her was knowing, bemused and loving. As though he knew but forgave.

She slowly lifted his hands up to the top of her corset and, after a shy glance at him, set them down. 'Please.'

Like someone unwrapping a precious gift, he slowly, carefully began unfastening her corset hook by hook. Once the corset was off, Anna was left wearing only the thin, sleeveless shift that went beneath it. She felt terribly exposed. It was a great relief to her when he lifted the bed sheets and indicated she slip in. In the blink of an eye, she was lying in his bed with the sheets pulled up to her chin.

Ivanovsky turned onto his side so that he faced her, and propped his head up with a cupped hand. 'You know, Anya, this is new thing for me too. I have only ever made love to a woman in Russian before.'

She met his solemn, drowsy-lidded eyes nervously. 'Is there a difference?'

'Before making love to woman's body, one must always first make love to her heart, her soul. It is strange to me to express such intimate feelings of my heart in your language. In English, such things sound trite; my heart cannot properly speak in this language. So—' He moved in close to her and brought his face to rest just above hers. 'You, sweetest, must learn some new words.'

She was sure her eyes had widened. English had always seemed to her a more than adequate tongue. Much better than any of the other barbarous tongues around, for sure. 'Oh.'

He smiled his warmest, most melting smile. 'Yes. *Ti takaya kraslvaya*, you are so beautiful. *Ti chudesnaya*, you are wonderful. *Ya tebya lyublyu*, I love you.' He started to place the gentlest kisses on her face and lips.

She was wrong, he was right. The Russian words contained love within their very sounds. They spoke directly to her heart. She felt herself melting under them. The love living in him, in his words, was so peaceful and deep. She allowed her heart to sink into them and her body to yield to his tender caresses.

'You will—' He paused to kiss her. 'Like this—' Another kiss. '*Eslib kazhdiy raz koda ya dumayu o tebe padala by zvezda, to luna stalaby odinokoy.*'

She let out a breathy sigh. 'It sounds beautiful. What does it mean?'

'Prodding mind is safely asleep?'

She giggled at the quietly teasing question and nodded. 'Russian sends it to sleep like a soothing lullaby.'

'It means—' A lingering kiss alighted on her lips. 'If star fell down every time I thought of you, moon would be lonely.'

'Oh...' she sighed, as feelings she had never allowed herself to feel warmed to life beneath his love.

He drew her shift off her shoulders and swept it down. Her arm moved instinctively to cover her nakedness, but his hand covered it already. The touch of his large fingers was reassuringly decided, yet gentle enough not to mark even the most delicate and tenderly swelling young flower bud.

'*Lyublyu tebya vsem sertdem, vsey dushoyu*, I love you with all my heart, all my soul,' he breathed, his eyes gazing deep into her own.

She felt a golden warmth spreading through herself before his love-filled words and gentle caresses. Their warmth reached into even the most frozen corners of her heart. Even the most lonely corners of her soul.

'Sasha...'

'Yes, my love?'

'I think I...love you...'

The mysterious, melting smile spread over his tender lips. He leaned down to place a kiss on her cheek. '*Ti mllaya*, you are sweet.'

She wrinkled her brow as she bit her lip hesitantly. 'Why do you not urge me to break with Mr Sleighman?'

He gently ran his fingers through her hair. 'I want you to follow your own path in freedom. Anya, if path you choose is the one he travels, this choice is yours to make.'

The furrows on her brow deepened. Part of her wanted him to beg her. Beg her to go with him. To throw himself before her and declare that he could not live without her.

'Why does my choice not pain you, Sasha?'

His face hovered just above her own, almost brushing it. She felt his soft, warm breaths on her cheek as he looked deep into her eyes. A profound sadness dwelt in their depths. 'Anya, it does hurt me. Because if you feel pain, I feel pain.'

She slowly reached her fingers up to his cheek and drew their quivering tips across his smooth skin. 'I do not wish to cause you pain…'

The depth of the tenderness living in his sad smile made the breath catch in her throat. '*Mllaya moyna*, my sweet, life is pain. That is why we must savour moments of happiness like this as children do; with no thought of what pain tomorrow will bring.'

Blinking hard, she nodded.

In a moment, the sadness had sunk below the dark surface. 'I see I have made you sad. Do not think of my pain. I am Russian, I like being melancholy.'

Anna pushed her lips into a smile, although she was sure his bleak joke had left its trace in the smile. 'Sasha, you are so beautiful…' she whispered, gently combing her fingers through his beguiling silver mane. Then her hands moved shyly over the warm, firm contours of his back.

'Anya, a Russian's beloved has many, many names...' he murmured, his lips brushing against her cheek as he spoke. 'Do you know all of your names...?'

'No,' she replied with an uncertain smile.

'Well...' His caressing hands travelled lingeringly over her body. 'They are *moy slavneey katyonak*, my sweet kitten, *doosha maya*, my soul, *maya neezhnaya dyevachka,* my tender girl, *solnishka*, little sun, *zayka maya*, my little rabbit, *lapooshka*, darling, and many more I have yet to bestow on you ...'

'Oh Sasha,' she gasped.

His caresses and kisses became more passionate and intimate. All the while, his tenderly murmured whispers of '*Ti takaya kraslvaya'* and '*Ta tebya lyublyu'* washed over her with a golden glory. Added to these words were a host of love-filled gasps of '*Moy slavneey katonak,*' 'Oh *doosha maya,*' 'Oh *zayka maya...*' and many more tender words he had yet to translate.

He did not need to translate them. The love they expressed spoke directly to her heart. Once he had carried her to the height of ecstasy, she floated in its lingering glow as she lay in his arms, her head resting on his firm, achingly masculine chest. She drunk in the warm, comforting scent of his skin and revelled at the feel of his fingers gently, almost absent-mindedly, stroking her hair.

Reclining back against the feather pillows, he reached for the cigar case sitting on the bedside table. 'Do you mind if I smoke?'

She gave a brief shake of the head, too filled with delicious indolence to speak.

Holding the thin cigar between his lips, he struck a match and drew in a breath as he held the flame up to the end of the cigar.

She observed the little ritual thoughtfully. To him it was clearly second nature, yet to her it was a novelty. What would it be like to be Mrs Ivanovsky and watch your husband striking that match and breathing out those clouds of sweetly aromatic blue smoke every evening?

He placed his free arm back around her shoulders and smiled lovingly down at her as he carefully blew the smoke out away from her face.

She looked up at him through lowered eyelashes. 'Do you always smoke in bed after making love to a woman?'

He rested a darkly melting sidewise glance on her as he breathed out a slow, smoky-blue breath. 'Always.'

Blushing slightly, she lowered her eyes.

He laughed softly. '*Ti takaya mllaya.*'

She giggled. 'No one else has ever called me sweet before.'

An exploring finger moved across her cheek. 'You are very *prelesnaya* too.'

'What does that mean?'

'*Prelesnaya* is cute.'

'Mabel and Mandy said I am a miserable starved-looking thing, and they are right. I am not cute,' Anna added firmly, shifting her head as she pouted a little.

'Yes you are, *lapooshka.*'

'Not.'

'Are.'

But before she could answer, she let out an involuntary little shriek as his fingers brushed over the most ticklish spot under her arm. 'No, Sasha, stop it!' she giggled.

'See there, you have the most adorably cute dimples on your cheeks when you laugh.'

She sighed happily. 'No one has ever told me that.'

'That is likely because hardly anyone else has ever seen you laugh.'

A few minutes of companionable silence later, she lifted her head a little. 'Sasha, can I try that?'

'Certainly, *mllaya moyna*.' He held out his slowly smouldering cigar. 'But mind you do not breathe in much.'

She drew in a mouthful of the sweetly aromatic smoke. And a moment later was spluttering heartily while tears ran down her cheeks and Sasha laughed gently at her.

'You were warned, Miss I-know-Best.'

'Gosh, that *is* strong,' she gasped.

He took the cigar back and drew a mouthful of smoke.

Once she had settled her head comfortably back onto his chest, he held her close. 'Anya, Was it good for you? I did not hurt you?'

The sensitive, quietly uttered question still made Anna blush and lower her eyes bashfully. 'Yes it...was—' she felt the blush deepen, 'very pleasurable.'

'Good, I am very happy you are satisfied,' came his slowly murmured reply.

During the peaceful silence that then reigned for a while, the lone candle reached its last half-inch and started to flicker and gutter fitfully. The faint light of the dying candle was now out-shone by the silver moonlight tiptoeing in through the window.

'Sasha...'

Yes, *doosha maya*...?' came his drowsy response.

'What do you think happiness is?'

'Tell me what *you* think it is,' was his only slightly more alert answer.

'Happiness is being respected by one's peers and being able to hold one's head up high in society. It is enjoying a comfortable and dignified lifestyle befitting to one's station in life. That is what I think happiness is.'

A breath of wind that stirred the curtain as it crept in through the window blew out the candle's fading flame with a low sigh.

'What most people think of as happiness is an ephemeral and unimportant thing,' came his quiet reply. 'Being at peace within yourself is much more valuable. True contentment is peace of knowing that you have passed through suffering without breaking. Peace is when you know you have done well. It is when you are at peace with yourself, at peace with life, with the world around you.'

'So are you saying that you cannot be happy unless you suffer?'

'Yes. Deep, profound contentment is quiet thing. It is what soul feels when it has passed through purging flames of suffering, because suffering strengthens and purifies the soul. Soul can only be at peace when it is pure.'

Not long after, his eyes fell shut and his breaths became a slow rhythm. But she remained awake long after Sasha had been enfolded in sleep's tender embrace.

The stillness of the night was broken only by a soft breeze sighing in the dusky, silver-showered garden, the distant, hushed murmur of the sea, and by her sleeping lover's low, gentle breaths.

Hour followed hour and still she sat silently gazing down on his moonlight-bathed face. The noble, deeply beautiful countenance was filled with such peace. Such purity. Such love. All through the night he slept the sleep of the blessed angels.

At last, a far off cockcrow heralded the coming dawn. Anna finally stirred. Silently, she leaned down over her sleeping lover and placed a single kiss on his brow.

Then, like a ghost before the coming daylight, she was gone.

8

Why Have You Misted Over, Clear Sunset?

ANNA was just macerating the last mouthful of toast and marmalade when her bedroom door was flung open.

'Knock, would you!' she shouted, without turning to see who it was.

'N, I must speak with you.'

Anna glared up at her sister, who stood grimly at the foot of the bed. 'But I have not even got up! You know I cannot bear to be plagued early in the morning.'

Jennifer gave the clock a withering look. Its arms stood at ten. '*Early.* I think not. Only matrons may respectably lounge at their breakfast in bed at this hour.'

Anna let out a huff of annoyance. 'What do you want, Jen?'

'I'm afraid that Mr Sleighman has brought certain concerns to my attention.'

Tea slopped onto the saucer as the hand holding the teacup wobbled violently. The defiance drained from its holder's face in an instant. 'Concerns?'

'Yes, concerns.' Jennifer fidgeted with the corner of her shawl, and after a moment's tense silence, sat down on the edge of the bed. 'He says you sometimes behave towards him in a manner that is slightly callous, that you—that you appear to take pleasure in causing him to feel uncomfortable. He also drew to my attention the fact that you are rather cold towards him, lacking the warmth which a man has the right to expect from his fiancée.'

Anna set her teacup down very carefully, her lips tight with anger. After all she had let him do. She did not reply.

'Well?' demanded Jennifer.

'Well what?'

Jennifer's face tightened. 'What have you got to say for yourself?'

'I really have nothing to say for myself,' Anna replied as nonchalantly as she could. 'He is quite right, I am a cold fish. And you know I do not love him, so why should I gush affection over him? You said yourself that love is of no importance when entering into marriage.'

'I warrant it, Mr Sleighman is indeed being rather demanding to expect so much of you. But it is your duty to please the man, so I suggest you quit your habit of toying with him like a kitten toying with a mouse!'

Anna looked defiantly back at her sister. 'Why should I?'

'Because you do not wish to end your days as a bitter old maid!'

'Mr Sleighman knew what I was like when he asked Father for my hand; he has no right to suddenly expect me to change my manner!'

'Beggars can't be choosers, Anna! If you had cast off that glacial, subtly contemptuous manner you are so fond of, then perhaps you might have made a match more pleasing to yourself. I suggest that you stop having such a bad grace about you; you only have yourself to blame!'

Anna knew her sister had a point. Gentlemen favoured sweet, meek creatures who sang prettily as they hopped about in their gilded cages, not pecking, resentfully sullen magpies. Except for Ivanovsky. He seemed very taken with scruffy-feathered magpies.

'Anna, you know that duty done is the root of all happiness,' said Jennifer, more calmly. 'Having an unmarried daughter who is the cause of gossip brings shame upon the family. You know you have no choice but to marry Mr Sleighman.'

Anna's heart leapt sickeningly within her. 'Gossip?'

'Mother said in her letter that you danced a little too much with some man at a ball, and it started some silly rumour. It is quite ridiculous, I mean, you dancing wantonly with some unsuitable pauper like a wild rebel!'

'Quite!' Anna laughed nervously. Her face felt hot. 'The gentleman in question meant nothing to me—I doubt I would even recognise the man if I met him again!' she added with another nervous laugh, anxiously feeling her cheek as if that would tell her how red it was.

Jennifer smiled tightly. 'Indeed. The thought of you forming a passionate attachment is quite ludicrous.' Then her expression turned grim once more. 'I must return to the purpose I came here for. Will you treat poor Mr Sleighman with more care?'

Anna over-carefully put her empty breakfast tray onto the bedside table and slowly lifted up her teacup. She knew she had just taken on the glacial expression that Jennifer held responsible for so much. But she did not care.

'If he treated me with more care, I should gladly do so,' she replied coldly.

Jennifer's hands jerked up angrily. 'What are you talking about? Mr Sleighman is a delightful, sweet man!'

As Anna looked away, she drew frosty aloofness more tightly about herself. 'I do not like the way he imposes on my person.'

'Who are you to talk?' cried Jennifer, pointing fiercely at her sister. 'You struck the poor man in the face before his neighbours and future in-laws!'

Anna felt her façade of ice begin to crack, and a sudden terror that she might cry seized her. But she was too hurt and angry to be silent. 'I could have been killed, and I felt such a fool sprawled on the floor like that in front of everyone!'

'Mr Sleighman was unwise not to allow Mr Ivanovsky to aid him, but it was an accident. The poor man did not mean to drop you, and you saw how grieved he was!'

Anna set her teacup and saucer down with a crash. 'He lugged me like a sack of sugar!'

Jennifer stood up with a decisive jerk and wagged a finger at

Anna. 'I will have no more said against poor Mr Sleighman! It is clear to everyone but you that the man is besotted with you and would never do anything to hurt you. He is an excellent catch for you, so stop this ungrateful nonsense!'

Blinking hard, Anna miserably drew her knees up towards her chin. She kept her head turned firmly away, and resentment churned inside her. 'I reserve my right not to be besotted with the man.'

'Oh good for you! You really are such a spoilt child. You do realise that you only have yourself to blame for being dropped on the floor?'

Anna turned towards her sister like a poked adder. 'What, because I am too heavy?'

'No,' replied Jennifer, in a tone that suggested she was deploying every bit of patience she possessed. 'Because you were making a fool of yourself with that Russian.'

The most horrible fear Anna had ever felt closed around her. What if Jennifer—someone, *anyone*—knew? The gossip bred by that night at the ball would seem like a little girl's tea party compared with being shamed as a fallen woman. The fear squeezed hard.

Words came tumbling up before she could think. 'Did I flirt? Did I laugh and talk excessively? No! I merely had a normal conversation with a gentleman who is a guest in *your* house!' she shouted back savagely.

Jennifer cleared her throat and smoothed her mousy-brown, tightly scraped-back hair. Then she looked at Anna as one might an elderly relative who is a few cards short of a full deck. 'I agree that you neither flirted nor made an exhibition of yourself, but it was not a *normal* conversation.'

Anna's mind scrabbled wildly, frantically searching for anything that could have given her shameful act away. 'How do you know? You—you were not even there!'

Even though her plastered flat hair could not possibly get any flatter, Jennifer smoothed it some more. 'I saw you through the parlour window. It looks out onto the veranda, you know.' She turned away and walked over to the window. 'The exchange that you and Mr Ivanovsky had was clearly very intimate. The way you looked at each other, the frankness of your interaction…' Jennifer suddenly spun around to face Anna. 'It was not normal!'

'But that is merely Mr Ivanovsky's way!' Anna stammered desperately. 'He is Russian, he does not have that English reserve!'

'To be shockingly informal is one thing, but to converse like a pair who have been intimately acquainted for a hundred years is quite another! Jennifer had now advanced to the foot of the bed once again. 'The cruelty on your part was that you stepped out from behind your frosty, haughty barricade; you never do that for poor Mr Sleighman! To almost everyone but that Russian, you act as though they are pins sticking into the suffering wretch that is you! And don't think that pantomime you put on at the dinner party fooled me as it did Mr Sleighman's fond heart. You resented even his glance!'

Although Anna's heart still thudded against her chest uncomfortably, its rhythm had slowed. If Jennifer had any evidence more damning than an overly intimate conversation and some frank eye contact, she would have deployed it by now.

Anna calmly leaned back against the headboard and eyed her

sister coldly. 'I admit that I find some social intercourse tiresome, but I did not invite Mr Ivanovsky's informality, nor did I welcome it. That Mr Ivanovsky has a talent for drawing one forth into his confidence is no fault of mine. I persist in my opinion that Mr Sleighman had no genuine cause to be jealous.'

'You do not resent Mr Ivanovsky's glance. That is quite clear.' Jennifer closed her hands tightly around the railing of the bed frame. 'No. You welcome it; beneath it you unfurl your petals like a daisy beneath the sun!'

Anna nervously put her cup and saucer on the bedside table. It was an excuse to turn from her sister's steely eyes for a moment. A chance to compose herself. Jennifer was much too close to the truth for comfort. Anna cursed herself for her carelessness that hot afternoon on the veranda.

'It is undeniable that Mr Ivanovsky is possessed of a more comely appearance than Mr Sleighman, and also a greater charm of address and deportment—' Anna stopped for a moment to swallow, hoping that would clear her voice of its wobble. 'Ahem, it is not entirely incorrect to presume that I find Mr Ivanovsky a more engaging companion than Mr Sleighman, but that is of no importance. You know quite well that I am not some foolish, over-excitable young girl whose only aim in life is to fall in love. You can rest assured, Jen, that I shall do my duty by this family.'

Jennifer removed her hands from the bed frame and carefully wiped them on her skirt. 'I am most pleased that you express this virtuous sentiment. But—' She suddenly looked up at Anna. 'You have always had a kind of resentment about you. It is not rebellion, but it is the *seed* of rebellion. Mind you neither push it into fertile earth nor pour water onto it.' And with that grim warning ringing in the room, Jennifer strode out and slammed the door behind her.

Anna hugged her knees tight and rested her chin on them as she stared bleakly at the wall. Ivanovsky's mere presence was deeply fertile earth. As for his words... She gazed out at the blue ocean shimmering under the bright summer sun. His words were showers of sweet, gentle rain more copious than the ocean lapping at these pale sands.

'I shall do my duty by this family,' she whispered to herself. 'I shall do my duty by this family, I shall do my duty by this family...'

* * * *

Anna looked to her sunbonnet, which set on her dresser. For the tenth time in the past half hour, she picked it up. This time, she did not put it back down again.

'Stop hiding in a hole like a hunted animal, Anna,' she said aloud to herself. 'You are a young woman of considerable means, not a cowering mouse.'

With her nerves bolstered by this little talking-to, she crept for the door. The thought of meeting either Mr Sleighman or Ivanovsky was unbearable. She could not shake off the irrational fear that her secret would be out if Jennifer or Mr Sleighman saw her and Ivanovsky together. How could she ever meet Ivanovsky's gaze in public again?

'You have nothing to fear, because you shall do your duty by your family,' she repeated to herself determinedly.

Then Anna opened her door and peered out. She scanned left, she scanned right, but all was quiet in the hallway. After one last look around, she stepped out and shut the door behind her. With light, soundless footfalls, she crept swiftly down the hall. But just as she was beginning to breathe again, a door jerked open.

'Come and see my drawing, Anna!' cried Mabel.

Anna froze. The door Mabel peered forth from was Ivanovsky's.

'Ahmm, ahmm...I really haven't the time. I am going for a walk, you see,' she replied shakily.

'Yeah, you've got to see,' came Mandy's voice from within. 'Mabel's been working wretchedly hard all day on it.'

Anna cleared her throat nervously. 'But—but—'

Before Anna could finish, Mandy had marched out and seized her arm.

'Mandy, I truly cannot spare the time!'

Anna's protests were ignored. Before she could think of any more weighty excuses, Mandy had towed her along the hallway to Ivanovsky's open door.

'Really, Mandy, I do not have time!' Anna gasped desperately.

The only reply this latest protest received was a firm push from behind that sent her staggering into the room.

While Anna was still occupied with attempting to regain her scattered wits and upset balance, a gentle, assured hand closed supportively around her arm, and the deep, soft scent of cologne, held close by the golden summer air, enveloped her senses. A moment later, a bare lower arm brushed against her own naked skin, and a warm, gentle breath sighed against her cheek.

Her senses leapt with recognition, and with memories of happiness and pleasure. Every sense except two. One she would not allow the delight it craved, and the other she prayed would not receive the caress it pleaded for.

'Anya, are you alright?'

She could not look up. Could not. A stifled gasp that had tried to be a sob escaped her. The simple peace and tenderness of his voice was torment. Then he took her other hand in his. She knew he was standing in front of her.

'Mundushka, to startle Miss Anya so is unkind; you ought to let her do things as she wishes.' Even though this was a reprimand, it was so kindly spoken that it sounded not at all like one.

Anna wanted to cry.

Her hand received a gentle squeeze. '*Doosha maya?*'

His lovingly concerned murmur was too much for Anna. She looked up. His heavy-lidded brown eyes had never looked so tender, so love-filled. Then he smiled. She felt a burning blush spread over her cheeks. His smile became wider before he hastily looked down. Anna's cheeks grew hotter still. Turning quickly away, she slipped her hands free and hurried over to the window.

'Look, Anna!'

'Yeah, you have to come and see!'

Hastily arranging her face into an expression suitable for polite society, Anna noticed the twins for the first time since she had entered the room. Mabel sat at a table, and Mandy stood behind her. Both of them were looking squarely at Anna.

She had to fight hard to retain the casual, amiable little smile she had so carefully moulded her lips into. After clearing her throat awkwardly, Anna made her way across to the glowingly enthusiastic Mabel and Mandy.

She kept her eyes firmly down as she crossed the floor. Just one glimpse of Ivanovsky would be all the advantage the emotions heaving within needed to storm her mannerly façade.

When Anna arrived, Mabel held up a large sheet of paper. 'Look at my drawing!'

Anna looked. A detailed drawing in coloured pencil met her eyes. The skill of the artist was notable. But not as notable as the subject. The object at its centre was instantly recognisable as the chaise-lounge placed before the window she had been standing at only moments ago. Sitting on a low footstool before it was Mandy. And artistically draped over the chaise-lounge was—Ivanovsky.

Anna's heart leapt up, and her eyes almost followed it. But she forced them back onto the paper. At least his likeness in pencil could not look back at her, could not smile *that* smile.

Mabel had drawn him with one leg casually stretched out on the chaise and the other resting on the floor. A sketching pad lay forgotten in his lap. He posed chin in hand, his elbow resting easily on the chaise-lounge's arm. She knew enough about art to know that this gesture was the traditional representation of melancholy. The expression of the sitter's face only added to the effect. He held the viewer's eyes with a contemplative gaze of gentle, quiet sadness.

'Its—its delightful, Mabel!' Anna gushed uncertainly. 'How very clever you are!'

'What don't you like about it?' said Mandy, without looking up.

'Yeah, what?' echoed Mabel.

'It's perfectly lovely, except—' Twisting her hands nervously together behind her back, Anna paused for a moment. 'Except that Mr Ivanovsky looks awfully cheerless. Quite bleak, in fact!'

'Mabya, Miss Anna might have worthy point. I am quite sure I did not wear such a melancholy face when I posed for you earlier.'

Anna thought she felt a gentle breath stir her hair. Ivanovsky sounded as though he stood close enough behind her. Then again, perhaps it was only the breeze sighing in through the open window.

'You are right,' declared Mandy. 'But so is Mabel.'

'Yeah, just so. You did look appropriately sunny when you sat for me, Sasha. But we've seen you sitting on the root of that old willow down by the stream which you pass on your walk every morning.'

'Just so. We're early birds; nothing that goes on around here is missed by us.'

'Yeah, we see everything.'

'Not like *her*,' added Mabel, casting a sideways glance at Anna.

'Before the sun is up, we see you sitting on that gnarly old willow root singing some sad little song, or just looking woefully out at the stream.'

'I like to sit and just ponder,' Ivanovsky replied rather bashfully.

Cursing herself soundly, Anna pulled her eyes away from him. There was something about that slightly bashful smile that was desperately endearing. She could not trust herself in its presence.

'What do you think about?' Mandy asked loudly.

'Yeah, what?'

A pensive sadness descended upon Ivanovsky's face like soft evening mist upon a shadowy vale. 'I am far from home, I miss the love of those dear to me. I miss my native land, the scent of her air, the beauty of her song, the voices of her children. And sometimes my heart, it yearns for the presence of a love that cannot bring itself to approach...'

Anna suddenly choked. As she coughed and spluttered heartily, she hastily moved over to the window with a handkerchief held to her lips.

She heard some whispers and giggles from the twins, and a hushed but firm rebuke from Ivanovsky. Then there was a moment's silence. Anna was cringing desperately. She could not turn towards them.

'Anna, why don't you come and draw something with us?' asked a repentant young voice.

'But I am terrible at drawing,' Anna replied, without turning around.

Memories of her frustrating attempts to sketch the seascape irked her. The tumbling, many-mooded ocean had defied all her desires to capture its wild, fearful beauty. Her meagre artistic skills had caused the attempts to end with Anna angrily snapping her pencil in half and tossing both it and the sketching pad aside. She had long since outlawed all drawing, however much of a desirable feminine accomplishment it might be considered.

'Paint something then.'

Anna turned slightly towards the table. But only slightly. 'It has been years since I painted anything. I am sure I have quite forgotten how to.'

'Sasha will help you.'

'Yeah, Sasha will help you.'

Anna did not want Sasha to help her with anything. She hesitated awkwardly.

'Come on!' called Mabel.

'Yeah, stop shilly-shallying.'

Anna slowly made her way over to the table, keeping her eyes fixed on the floor the whole time.

One of the twins—Anna could not see which—pulled out a chair. A sheet of gleaming white paper was thrust in front of her.

Anna carefully sat down. Mabel and Mandy sat down too. Anna did not know where Ivanovsky stood. All she knew was that she could not see him from where she sat providing she kept her eyes down. This was good enough. Mabel shoved an open box of watercolour paints over, and Mandy pushed a paintbrush into Anna's hand.

Anna stared fearfully down at the shining white paper. 'I don't know what to paint.'

'Paint anything you fancy.'

'I don't fancy anything.'

Mandy giggled, but it quickly turned into a squeal when Mabel poked her with a pencil.

Mabel kept her unwilling face determinedly straight. 'A sunrise is good to paint.'

'Yeah, paint a sunrise,' Mandy echoed, her face a picture of forced seriousness.

'But I have no sunrise to copy,' Anna protested weakly.

'You don't need one to copy,' replied Mabel. 'Everyone knows what a sunrise looks like.'

'Mind you, Anna's probably never seen one,' chirped Mandy.

Mabel frowned. 'I hadn't thought of that.'

'Paint a *sunset* then,' said Mandy.

'Yeah. They look much the same anyway,' added Mabel.

'I beg to differ.'

Anna started at the sound of Ivanovsky's voice coming from right behind her. She suddenly felt sure that he was resting a hand on the back of her chair.

'Sunset never feels same as sunrise. If one cannot tell the difference between painter's sunrise and sunset, painter needs to improve.'

Anna's throat tightened, but she dared not move. She had to paint if she was to avoid further embarrassment. Tightening her fingers around the brush nervously, she shakily dipped it into the water jar, then dipped it into one of the colours in the paintbox.

She put little thought into her selection of colours. All she cared about was covering the blank white paper glaring challengingly up at her. When Anna heard Ivanovsky stir and move away, she breathed a little easier.

After hastily, carelessly slopping colour on for a while, Anna paused. Out of the corner of her eye, she glimpsed Ivanovsky sitting at the window seat with his folded arms resting on the windowsill and his head cradled on them. His gaze was far away, and his soft, full lips pensively parted. She quickly returned her attention to the paper before her.

But just as Anna began to work once more, a softly hummed tune reached her ears.

Mabel looked up from her drawing. 'What song is that, Sasha?'

'It is *Shto Zatumanilas.*'

'Is that the one about the man who must depart from his sweetheart?' asked Mabel.

The humming unfolded into song.

Why have you misted over, clear sunset,
Have you fallen onto the earth with the dew?
Why have you become lost in thought, lovely maiden?
Do your eyes shine with tears?

Sadly, I must part from you, my dark-eyed maiden,
The cock has struck his wings.
Soon it will be midnight...

The song faded back into a sadly hummed melody, then, after a few couplets, rose into words once more.

Is it my fault that I love thee, my dark-eyed maiden,
More than my very soul?
More, ah! than my very soul!

When Ivanovsky's voice faded at last, Anna paused and looked up from her painting. Mandy and Mabel looked grimly back at her.

Anna looked quickly down again. And for the first time, she noticed what her painting looked like. Her attempt at rolling hills had turned out a confused chaos of lumpy, liverish brown shapes. The pale blues and lilacs she had tried to make into an evening sky had been so swamped by the running, bleeding browns that they turned a muddy, nondescript shade of brown-grey. As for the setting sun, its golden yellow also had been suffocated by the all-pervading liverish brown, and had mixed further with the blue, resulting in a dark, sickly, brownish green. The only clear colour to be found dwelt in the very centre of the sun's golden orb.

Anna sighed fretfully. It was awful—no, it was *worse* than awful. It was unspeakably hideous.

In desperation, she loaded her brush with bright violet and plastered it over what ought to have been the sky. Then she put aside her brush and surveyed the results.

They were not pleasing. In fact, if anything, it had made things worse. The colour that glared back at her reminded her of something. She frowned at it some more. Yes, it was the very same shade as that frightful dusky angel's strange eyes.

If Anna had been alone, she would have gasped with the horror of it. Quickly, she thrust the still-damp sheet aside.

She sighed wearily. 'Mabel, I told you I cannot paint or draw. I wish I had not let you frightful imps bully me into trying. Everything I paint ends up looking like nothing. That is all I ever paint: nothing.'

'I told you to get Sasha to help,' replied Mabel.

'Yeah, you should have.'

'I am telling you, I have not one single artistic bone in my entire body. I very much doubt that even the greatest master could teach a student as wretchedly talentless as me anything at all.'

'The gauntlet has been tossed, and I accept.'

Anna looked up with a start. Ivanovsky stood smiling down on her. She quickly lowered her eyes. 'I would not wish to subject anyone to such a hopeless pupil.'

'I believe you are neither talentless nor hopeless, Miss Anya.'

She jerked her hand at the hateful painting before her. 'But I am! Look at it!'

The soft scrape of a chair being drawn out sounded from right beside Anna. She determinedly shielded her face with her hand and pushed her own chair a little further in the opposite direction.

'No artist has ever painted "nothing", I assure you,' came his quiet response.

She drew back sullenly. 'Trust me, I have.'

'What I believe you mean to say, darling, is that your paintings do not have appearance of anything one can see with physical eyes. That, however, does not mean they depict "nothing".'

Without noticing what she was doing, Anna slapped her shielding hand down on the table and eyed Ivanovsky crossly. 'What are you talking about?'

He faced her with patient good humour. 'Artists often paint feelings, thoughts and experiences that live within their souls, not physical matter.'

'Oh, I see.'

She looked at her painting again. The evening sky was her:

swamped, dirtied and suffocated by the towering, virulent mass that was Mr Sleighman, her family, the society in which she lived. She was not sure what the sun was. Perhaps it was something true and pure at her very core. Whatever it was, its survival was precarious.

With sudden violence, Anna seized the painting, tore it in half and threw the fragments on the ground.

Then she turned to Ivanovsky. 'Teach me how to paint something beautiful.'

'Gladly.' He placed a clean sheet of paper before her. 'The rainbow is Mother Nature's painting, so it is natural place for us to begin.'

Anna picked up a graphite pencil. 'How do I begin?'

'By putting down that pencil.'

She tightened her grip on it. 'But my watercolour paintings end up a mess if I do not draw the outlines first.'

He drew his chair in a little closer. 'If painter draws too many lines, colours become boxed in.'

'Precisely. It stops them rampaging wildly about.'

He smiled and shook his head. 'Colours do not enjoy being boxed in by dark lines. Artist must let them interact, talk with each other, intermingle, *embrace*.'

Anna pointed a scathing finger at the torn scraps lying at her feet. 'But they are hideous when they intermingle!'

Ivanovsky was clearly unperturbed. 'How does hostess seat guests when she has dinner party?'

Anna folded her hands thoughtfully together in her lap. 'She seats the guests next to other guests with whom they will have interesting and agreeable conversation, I suppose.'

'Exactly. Artist must do likewise. Some colours, they do not get on, and others, they have nothing interesting to say to one another.'

'I see.'

Slowly and patiently, with quietly murmured directions and the occasional gentle guiding touch on Anna's hand, a clear, glowing rainbow came into being on the paper.

When it was finished, Anna gazed on it in quiet satisfaction. It might be simple, but it was beautiful and she had created it with her own hands. Somehow, the fact that she had created something pure and beautiful made her feel less stained and miserable.

Mabel and Mandy quickly crowded around the new painting.

'See, we told you Sasha could show you how,' declared Mandy.

'Totally, just so.'

Anna felt the hand of Ivanovsky, who had arisen to make room for the twins, touch lightly on her shoulder. 'The white birch tree never fails to bud in spring.'

Anna frowned. 'What does that mean?'

'It means,' said Mabel, 'that things never fail to grow and develop under the right conditions.'

Anna furrowed her brow thoughtfully. 'Indeed.'

'Sasha, where is your gum eraser? asked Mandy, glancing up from the drawing she had just started.

'In the bedside cabinet,' he replied.

Anna got up. 'I'll fetch it. Which drawer is it in, Sasha?'

'It is beside my cigar case.'

Anna opened the top drawer and picked up the eraser. But when she turned back to the twins, she found them looking at her rather triumphantly.

'How did you know where he keeps his cigar case?' asked Mandy, in the tone of one examining a witness.

'Because I saw him put it there, of course.'

'I thought you had never been in here,' said Mabel.

Anna searched frantically for a suitable lie. 'I—I...' Then she gave up. It was no use. 'I have been in here to visit Mr Ivanovsky on one occasion, yes.'

Four raised eyebrows greeted this admission.

'What is so interesting about that?' snapped Anna.

With one synchronised motion, the twins turned to Ivanovsky, who stood before the window. His eyes were lowered, and Anna thought she detected a height of colour on his cheeks that was not usually there.

'You only ever smoke in—' began Mabel.

'Bed,' finished Mandy.

Smiling guiltily, he looked away.

The four wide blue eyes shifted back to Anna. The verdict was clear and unanimous.

In an instant, Anna's cheeks were aflame. 'What? No, how dare you!'

Then she fled.

9

Already the Fog Has Descended

ANNA'S fingers sifted franticly through the drawer's contents. Every bottle she found was seized and held up for closer inspection. But when it failed to contain the words *laudanum*, *opium*, *sleeping potion*, or *cold remedy*, it was thrown back in disgust. The drawer emitted a loud screech as it was slammed shut.

Then its next-door neighbour was roughly hauled open and the search began anew. This drawer was crowded with perfume bottles, gloves, hairpins and other assorted feminine paraphernalia. With a huff of frustration, Anna suddenly pulled the drawer out completely and turned it upside down so that everything tumbled out onto the floor. Then, dropping to her knees, she started rifling through the drawer's late contents.

'N, what in heaven's name are you doing?'

Anna's hands froze and her head lifted with a start. 'I am looking for an, ahem, an embroidery—a pink embroidery thread!'

'Well you will not find any thread in my dressing table drawers, I can assure you.' Jennifer now stood before the crouching Anna with her hands on her hips. 'What an awful mess you have made!'

Anna slowly rose to her feet. 'I am terribly sorry, Jen. I really did get frightfully carried away just there.'

Scowling sourly, Anna's sister stirred the jumbled mess with her foot. 'Really, N, you must learn to control that dreadful impetuous temper of yours.'

'I'll go and see if there is any thread in…in my own dresser…' muttered Anna, drifting fugitively towards the open door.

But she had barely moved two steps when Jennifer seized her elbow. 'Do not go away!'

Anna stopped, but did not turn her head.

'Mr Sleighman is here,' said Jennifer. 'He is waiting for you in the parlour. Now get down there—and let us have none of your childish, selfish tantrums!'

Anna fixed into place her most innocent expression. 'I haven't the faintest idea what you mean to refer to.'

'Do not think you can fool me, N. I am perfectly aware of the horrid, cruel things you said to poor Mr Sleighman on Tuesday after the tennis party!'

Anna tossed her head haughtily and maintained a frosty silence.

'Mr Sleighman is waiting!'

'You know, Jen, I feel sure I am coming down with a cold,' said Anna, her haughtiness now replaced by her best wilting flower impression. 'I don't suppose you happen to have any sore throat medicine knocking about here?'

Jennifer bent down and picked a brown glass bottle up from the heap at her feet. 'Here.'

Anna made no move to take the offered object. 'That medicine does nothing for me.' She coughed pitiably and felt her forehead with a drooping hand. 'I am quite sure that the most dreadful cold is coming on. I really ought to be seen by Dr Bramell.'

'Nonsense! You really are the most dreadful hypochondriac! Now off you go to see poor Mr Sleighman.'

With a sigh of defeat, Anna moved off. She dragged her feet all the way to the parlour door. Before she opened it, she stopped at the hall table. A tray with a bottle of gin on it sat there. All alone.

Anna looked about. Yes, all alone. She unscrewed the cap, brought the cool glass rim to her lips and gulped. Then she gulped again and again before putting it down. With her hand on the doorhandle, Anna paused yet again.

She had not seen Mr Sleighman since he had dropped her at the foot of the stairs two days previously. Why could not Mr Sleighman stay away for another two? Or better still, forever?

Anna almost slapped herself. What a ridiculous thought. She was fast approaching thirty. She had to marry, and marry soon. No man wanted to wed some withered old woman who had flouted her wares in vain for the past twelve years. Not unless the man was as desperate as Mr Sleighman was.

After giving her mouth a tired wipe with the back of her hand, Anna opened the parlour door and swept in.

Mr Sleighman arose from his chair immediately and hurried towards her. He narrowly avoided stumbling over the ottoman in the centre of the room.

'How're you, Anna, how're you?' he muttered nervously.

Anna coldly stepped back from his outstretched arms and puckered lips. 'I am well, thank you, Mr Sleighman.'

Clutching his hands uncertainly together and shifting softly from foot to foot, he kept his eyes lowered against her stabbingly direct gaze. 'You need to call me Norris like I asked, Anna.'

'I prefer to avoid lazy, uncouth informality, Mr Sleighman.'

His shifting became faster, and his chest caved in some more. 'But—but—but you call *him* that.'

'I am not aware that I refer to anyone of my acquaintance by that name?' Anna replied with fake innocence.

Mr Sleighman's eyelid twitched, and he nervously shuffled a little closer. 'That Russian—I'm talking about that—'

'Do you mean to refer to Mr Ivanovsky, Mr Sleighman?'

'Yes, yes, Sasha.'

Anna turned away. 'I have already answered that question for you once before, Mr Sleighman. You will forgive me if I decline to repeat myself.'

'Sorry...' Then there was an uncomfortable silence before he spoke again. 'Anna...I want to apologise again for dropping you like that. I shouldn't have done it.'

'Are you telling me that you dropped me on purpose, Mr

Sleighman?' she asked coldly, with her back still turned to him.

'No, of course not.'

With the regal air of a grand sailing ship, Anna slowly turned around to face him. 'What is it you are apologising for then, Mr Sleighman? Lifting me up in the first place? Being a puny shadow of a man? Pushing Mr Ivanovsky's offer of help aside?'

Although she had not thought it possible, his shoulders sunk inwards some more. 'I don't know...'

'Indeed.'

'With a woman, you never know what you've done to upset her, so it's best just to apologise regularly,' he replied with an awkward giggle. Then he waited hopefully for her to laugh.

Anna just tightened her lips.

Mr Sleighman suddenly snatched something up off the ottoman and gleefully held it out to her. 'These are for you!'

Anna looked down at the wilted flowers with contempt, and moved out a reluctant hand to take them. 'Oh, lovely.'

'I'm so glad you like them! I spent ages picking them on the way.'

She wrinkled her nose at the stingingly bitter smell arising from the white sap oozing from the bruised stems. 'Indeed. The puha stalks are quite delightful.'

Her sarcasm was lost on him. Relief flooded his face. 'You'd better put them in water.'

'Yes, before they decompose completely.'

'Have you had a good day?'

She was silent for a moment. Her day had been perfectly

ordinary. Ivanovsky had only been encountered briefly, and always in company. No word about the sweet night of love had been spoken. To her that night seemed like a distant dream. An experience so alien to her normal life that it bore no relation to reality.

She sighed. Nevertheless, it had been a heavenly dream. And when she closed her eyes, she could still feel his gently caressing touch and hear his tender, love-filled words. She smiled to herself. Russian really was a wonderful language…

'What's funny, Anna?'

She was dragged back from her dreamy thoughts to find Mr Sleighman smiling uncertainly up at her. 'Oh, nothing…I was merely thinking.'

'What were you thinking about? I want to know what you think about so that I can feel what you are feeling.'

Anna almost choked. If Mr Sleighman knew what she was thinking about, he would die of shock or go mad. Or go mad and *then* die of shock. 'Ahem, I, ahem, I was thinking about—as a matter of fact, it has quite slipped my mind now!' she answered, finishing with a nervous laugh.

'Oh, that is unfortunate.'

Anna busied herself with sticking the posy of weeds into a vase of roses sitting on the mantelpiece.

When she looked up from the completed task, she paused to study her reflection in the mirror above the fireplace. Her skin was now beyond delicately pale. It was ashen. And the bones it covered were becoming ever more pronounced. No, the months spent out here had not done her face any favours. She looked tired, haggard, strained. And the eyes...they were strangely hollow somehow. What eligible young Auckland bachelor would look at her now? No, not one man among them would look at a fading rose whose petals would be gone in the next gust of wind. Not when there were so many fresh new rosebuds unfurling their dewy petals all around.

'Your time is over, Anna,' she whispered to the pale reflection. 'There will be no new dawn for you...'

'What's that, Anna?'

'Nothing, Mr Sleighman, nothing at all,' she replied sadly, 'merely the wind tugging at the roses beneath the window.'

* * * *

The sky was covered by a fine veil of frothy high cloud. But for a determined few who kept up an erratic song, the cicadas were all silent, and there was a change in the wind. Its breath had cooled. No longer did it carry the stifling heat across the barren grasslands. The weathercock sitting atop Gravemore House had turned away from the northwest, and now tossed uncertainly from south to east.

Anna looked away from the weathercock and the skies spread out above it. She then lifted the hem of her voluminous dress and hurried forward.

One and a half hours of Mr Sleighman's conversation plus forty-eight hours of no sleep equalled hell. Ten more minutes of local politics, the price of sheep and the dangers of travel, and Anna felt sure she could have drawn and quartered him with a fruit knife. Opium. She was desperate for it. Nights without its stupefying embrace were torturous deserts bereft of all sleep and rest. Almost as torturous as meekly nodding and smiling at Mr Sleighman over an over-milky, over-sweet cup of tea while quietly screaming with boredom and annoyance inside. At least she would no longer have to pretend to find any of his conversation interesting when they were married. There was only one other thing that eased the torture, that filled the gaping emptiness. But it was forbidden. And far more dangerous than opium. Even thinking of it was dangerous and forbidden. So she roughly pushed it out.

Anna had now reached the banks of the stream that passed by Gravemore on its way to Aramoana Beach, where its waters united with the sparkling Pacific. With the back of her sleeve, she rubbed at her lips yet again. But it did not remove the feel of Mr Sleighman's wet goodbye kiss any more than her earlier attempts had. Rather, it brought to mind the words that had preceded it.

'That special moment under the stars will always live in our minds. It will be a romantic memory we'll never forget,' he had said, narrowing his eyes at her.

'What memory is that, Mr Sleighman?' she had replied.

'The first time I made love to you,' he had answered, in that manner he believed was so sweet and gratifying to young ladies.

Made love.

With a gasp, Anna hurried on faster, her hand held tightly over her mouth. Her stomach churned.

When she was in sight of Gravemore no longer, she stopped and looked out at the stream. Its peaceful waters rippled languidly beneath soft sunlight, and the weeping willows lining the banks further upstream dipped their roots in the river and trailed long green tresses into the cool, clear water. Reeds crowding the marshy margins chattered quietly amongst themselves, and the cry of an unseen bird came from some unseen place.

Anna parted the tall reeds and passed through, stepping out onto a large boulder at the stream's edge. There she crouched down and dipped her fingers into the water. As she did so, she looked across the whispering waters to where they slipped softly into the ocean like a child folding into the arms of a loving father. Returning to the being that gave rise to them, returning to the place from whence they came. Coming home.

Anna was desperate to return home too. Her heart longed for that joy. Unfortunately she did not know where home was— although Sasha Ivanovsky arms had felt more like one than any other place ever had. But that home was forbidden.

Lifting her eyes to where the blue sea touched the blue sky on the far distant horizon, she felt as though she would never leave this place. Auckland seemed so very far away now. Had it ever really existed at all? Perhaps it had just been a dream. This place was so remote, so alone, that it hardly seemed possible that any other place could exist.

She did not know why, but every time she gazed out over the deep blue sea, her eyes searched for a sail. A sail that would take her away from this place of torment. A sail would be coming over the horizon any day now. But it would not be taking her home. No. It would be carrying Sasha Ivanovsky out of her life forever. The only direction she would be going in was up the hill to the church. For her wedding day was on Saturday, and today was Thursday.

As if drawn by an invisible hand, Anna's head moved closer to the water slipping gently past at her feet. The golden pebbles lying at the bottom of the deep pool glistened in the sunlight that had broken through the clouds above. The clear water shimmered with a glittering glory, and silver bubbles floated and danced among it like jewels in a beauty's hair.

Her head dipped still closer. This little river was so joyful, so peaceful, so pure. It was going home.

Anna's hair now brushed the water's sparkling surface. If she joined it, she too could go home. She felt the cooling, soothing water caress her forehead. Its bright chatter seemed to change into an alluring, enticing whisper of invitation.

Yes, she could pass into its entrancing embrace and float down to join the brimming ocean. Finally she could answer the siren song of the waves. She could let the ocean carry away her pain, fill her emptiness and wash away the stains...

'I'm coming home...' she whispered, and let herself fall forwards.

Her face plunged into the cool water. The magic of the sparkling, shimmering underwater world was breathtaking. Nymphs of unearthly blues and greens frolicked all around. Sunbeams leapt and danced amongst them, and shone upon the pure, fresh green of the streaming underwater foliage.

With her eyes wide with wonder, Anna floated blissfully downwards. Then a dark, grinning form arose from the depths. Feathered black wings streamed behind it and its deep blue skin glimmered more enticingly than ever before.

'Come to me, my beloved...' murmured the dusky angel,

reaching out a darkly glinting hand to take hold of Anna's outstretched arms.

'Yes, take me...' she sighed, looking fearlessly into its wondrously hypnotic purple eyes. 'Take me...'

'Anya, no!'

No sooner had the cry sounded when Anna felt her downward descent come to a sudden stop. The nymphs and the dusky angel vanished in a flash, and her head suddenly resurfaced.

Anna coughed violently, but offered no resistance as she was pulled from the water by a painfully strong hand closed around her wrist. She then was roughly dragged back from the river's marshy edge.

Once under the spreading branches of the nearby willow, Ivanovsky threw away her hand. 'How could you? How, Anya?'

She shivered with the cold of the water that saturated her hair and dress and ran down her face. But more than that, she shivered at his anger. She had never before seen so much as one spark of anger in him. Now he stood with his head turned from her and a hand clasped over his eyes, as though looking at her was too painful.

She hung her head before his furious question. She felt so cold and afraid.

He turned to face her. A dark fire smouldered in the depths of his eyes. 'When there are still so many rays of hope in your life, how could you choose to shut them away? Why shut the lid on hope when all other evils unleashed by Pandora beset you?'

She shook her head dumbly. 'I don't know why I did it. All these sirens were calling to me—and—and I could not resist.' Suddenly she clutched her crawling head with numb hands. 'It is this place; I think I'm going mad!'

Terrible emotions burned in Ivanovsky's tortured face. There was deep pain, and perhaps more, but Anna could look no longer.

'You are coward, Anya! The path of your life has led into a shadowy vale of darkness and despair, but instead of having courage to scale towering cliffs that surround it so you might walk in light, you turn to vile creatures that dwell in its filthiest holes!'

'But the cliffs are too high for my feeble strength!'

'That is why I hold out my hand to you.'

'You know someone in my high position cannot take it without being shunned by society and disowned by their family! And besides, I am afraid of heights...'

'*Will* not. Someone in truly high position never needs dragging out of it.'

Then, after casting a look of the most pained disappointment on Anna, Ivanovsky turned to go.

Anna hurried desperately after him. 'Please don't take your love away from me!'

He did not stop or turn to look at her.

She seized hold of his arm. 'Please love me, Sasha, please!'

He stopped and slowly turned to her. 'What is it that your soul truly desires, Anya?'

Tears stung in her eyes and repressed sobs choked in her throat. She fell to her knees at his feet. 'I want you, Sasha!'

He crossed his arms like a barricade and determinedly turned away his head. 'You have me. You have always had me. But you will not submit to love when he is dressed so humbly, when he is without a golden crown upon his head and kingdom at his feet. You desire only to destroy yourself.'

She hung her head lower. 'I'm sorry; I don't know what came over me. It was like something was pulling me towards the water!'

'But you resisted not,' he replied bitterly.

A sob escaped her. 'I couldn't—just couldn't!'

'Wouldn't!' His head turned away further.

'Please, Sasha, please!' she sobbed, throwing her arms around his waist and clinging to him as tightly as a shipwrecked mariner clinging to the last life raft.

She sobbed against his unresponsive body. For him to turn his face from her felt like the sun turning its face from the earth.

His body remained rigid and unyielding. 'You will turn to vilest fiend before you will turn to me.'

She clung more tightly to him, sobbed louder and buried her face in the warm folds of his shirt. 'Can any crawling worm be more wretched than I? Please, Sasha, p-please love me!'

'I love you more than my very soul, Anya,' came his sad, distant reply. 'It is you who are too afraid to allow love to dwell in your heart...'

'But you know our love is doomed. It was doomed from the very beginning! We are creatures of opposite worlds, our love can never be!'

'Our love is doomed only because you choose to condemn it, dearest one,' he replied, his softly spoken words filled with bitter sadness.

'I condemn it because it must be condemned!' she sobbed. 'It is the kindest and the wisest thing!'

'As you will...'

Anna lifted her head to look up at him. His eyes were fixed on the softly murmuring river slipping past. He did not even seem to be aware of her clinging presence.

'Please Sasha, say that you understand, say that you forgive!'

But he did not reply, not in voice nor in glance.

Grief flooded her heart. Crying loudly, she clung to him with all her might. 'Please don't hate me!' she sobbed, with tears rolling down her cheeks like rain down a windowpane.

His body stirred, and a moment later he dropped to his knees. Tears veiled his eyes like the mists that dwell among the twilit winter forest.

He took her shaking hands in his and looked deep into her eyes with solemn earnestness. 'I will always love you. But if you desire to receive gift, dear one, you must hold out your open hand.'

'But you know that I cannot!' she sobbed despairingly.

A gentle patience dwelt in his sorrowful eyes. 'No, my beloved,' he replied in a low, trembling whisper, 'you cannot give to one what you have bestowed upon another.'

'But you do understand, don't you, Sasha?'

As though they were a veil drawn across heaven's infinite, wondrous reaches, his eyelids fell shut. He said nothing.

He did not understand. She knew he did not.

A torrent of tears that felt as unstoppable as the floods from the melting winter snows welled up. He could not understand, and now he would always be angry with her.

Then a gentle whisper reached her ear. 'Dry your eyes, dear one. I will forgive. I *do* forgive.'

She stopped mid-sob and looked up, as much in surprise as in relief. In his eyes, she could read his forgiveness as plainly as the astronomer might read the stars in the heavens.

'You do?'

'I do.'

She flung her arms around him, laid her head on his broad shoulder, and buried her face against his neck. 'I want you so much!' she gasped, sobbing as much with relief as she had been with grief but a moment ago. 'Know my heart is yours always, even if my hand is not.'

'You have me, *doosha maya*,' he replied softly. 'You have had me since moment I first saw your shadow.'

She lifted her head to look at the beloved face that now was so close to her. 'You are so wonderful that I know of no endearment I can call you that could possibly be worthy of you,' she whispered, holding his head between her shaking hands.

He held her gaze steadily. 'There is one thing only I ask of you, Anya.'

'Yes?' she asked uncertainly.

'Promise me you will never seek to end your life again.'

A promise freely given to a man of such profound integrity could not be broken. Anna thought hard. She did not want to give this pledge. But it was the only thing he had ever asked of her.

She finally looked up. 'I promise I will never seek to end my life.

I promise I will always have hope, even if it be only a little.'

With a sigh that seemed one of relief, he drew Anna towards him and enfolded her in a firm embrace. 'Thank you, Anya.'

After a few minutes of peaceful silence, Ivanovsky gently pushed Anna back.

'Shall I escort you back to house?' he asked, offering his arm.

She hesitated for a moment, feeling the loss of his embrace sorely. Then she placed her hand under the offered elbow. 'If anyone asks why I'm wet, I shall tell them that I lost my footing and slipped into the river. Do not tell them any different.'

* * * *

Early the next morning, Anna passed silently out of Gravemore's backdoor. Her skirts she lifted high to stop the dew that spangled the grass from soaking their hem.

Just before she passed out of sight of Gravemore's grimly staring windows, she paused and turned to look back. But no eyes had observed her passing.

The murmur of the river was a quick and lively one, but it was neither as quick nor as lively as the feet that traipsed lightly along its soft-grassed banks.

When Anna neared the old willow tree her feet slowed, but her heart quickened. After passing a tree fern, she had a clear view of the gnarled old willow.

Her heart leapt within her, for there, beneath the spreading boughs that had kept the damp dew away, was Sasha Ivanovsky. He was lying on his back with his knees drawn up, looking thoughtfully up at the green canopy and softly humming the tune *I am Travelling the Road Alone*. The first rays of the morning sun gilded the topmost leaves of the willow a shade of brighter green-gold and unseen birds greeted the new day with cheerful melody.

Anna came to an uncertain halt beside the cover bestowed by a generous sapling. She was beset by a vague fear that her coming would cause the enchanting scene to vanish if she stepped into it, like a fairy ring stepped into by a bumbling mortal. Or perhaps the peaceful scene would turn into a dreadful carnage, as it seemed did every scene she passed into. A dreadful tangle of tears, anguish, disappointment and strife.

But Anna did not have to find an answer, for it found her. She moved back a step so as to be better concealed, and in doing so startled a blackbird scratching among the leaf mould. Twittering its urgent alarm call, the bird fluttered noisily out and across the river. As one intimately acquainted with nature's voice, Ivanovsky naturally looked up to see who was there.

Not wishing to look like a spy or other such dishonourable lurker, Anna was forced to step forward. She did so with a nervous smile and a light step.

'Mr Ivanovsky, I do hope I am not disturbing you,' she said, and wished that she had sounded more self-assured.

Ivanovsky did not appear at all surprised to see her, although she did believe that she caught a colouring of worry in his warm, quiet smile of welcome. It was not unexpected. Her lonely presence by the river was hardly going to meet with joy from one who only yesterday had pulled her from its engulfing waters.

'Not at all, *Miss Brown*,' he replied, remaining lying.

This subtle comment on her formality was not lost on Anna. 'Sasha, forgive me...' she murmured uncertainly. 'I do not mean to be cold—to be so steely and miserable all the time.'

'I know this, *dragaya*. Why do you not sit?'

She hesitated for only a moment before sitting down beside him. But no sooner had she settled herself down when something beneath her was tugged on.

'Anya, darling, you might enjoy increased comfort if you were not sitting on my sketchbook. '

She lifted herself instantly. 'Oh gosh, do pardon me, I did not see it!'

His smile was gentle and reassuring. 'It is no matter. Both my person and my possessions are eminently robust.'

Anna gave a pained smile. Mr Sleighman's bumbling manner and social unease seemed to be catching. And to think that once she had been an elegant swan that glided around Auckland's grandest ballrooms. She could have cried.

'You still are.'

She frowned. 'I beg your pardon?'

'You still are a graceful swan,' he replied quietly, without looking up at her. 'Ruffled feathers soon smooth when less turbulent waters are sailed upon.'

She was both astonished and unnerved by this. She hardly knew what to say. Could he *really* be a mind reader? She regarded him cautiously from the corner of her eye. Those Russians really were an unnerving lot...

Suddenly, Ivanovsky laughed. Anna started violently.

His mysterious eyes now rested lightly upon her. 'The inhabitants of this place are a strange people; always finding terrifying magic where there is none and expecting genies to arise from every lamp they rub!'

Silently chiding herself for being such a silly child, Anna allowed her lips to smile, though she still only looked at him through cautiously lowered eyes. 'You are quite right, Sasha. I and my kind lack the obsession with the exotic, the mysterious and the occult which is such a feature of the more bohemian circles of society. We prefer to limit our concerns to homely, respectable matters becoming to God-fearing people.'

'Concerns such as imbibing laudanum, stealing from the poor to give to the rich, and silently going mad?'

Much as this reply irked her, Anna was determined not to be provoked. 'You must forgive such a domestic, little-travelled lady as myself for harbouring a mistrust of strange metaphysical phenomena. After all, who does not fear stepping blindly into an unknown void?'

'Perhaps if cautious lady were to remove her blindfold, the void would cease to be one and her step would not be blind one, but assured one.'

'Your words shall not sway me into any foolishness, however hard you might try,' Anna replied rather forcefully, a hint of frostiness creeping into her voice. 'I shall remain true to myself, and will let no one sway me!'

'Anya darling, you have many pretty words for saying you are coward.'

Somewhere deep down, she knew he was right. But she did not want to admit this. So she said nothing, and hung her head miserably.

Anna felt a gentle hand on her arm. 'Oh dearest one, do not be sad. It is hard to be brave.'

She looked down bashfully before his directness. When she looked up, an uninvited smile made an appearance on her lips.

His direct gaze turned subtly teasing. 'Tell me.'

She felt her cheeks warm, and modesty forced her eyes down again. 'Tell you what?'

'Tell me your thoughts.'

She felt her cheeks grow warmer still. She could not have looked up if she had wanted to.

'Stop blushing and tell me,' he demanded laughingly.

Embarrassed as she was, she could not help her smile growing wider. 'No, Sasha! Maidenly modesty forbids me.'

'I dare you to defy her.'

She collapsed beneath his teasing. 'The thing is, Sasha, I—I—'

She felt a cajoling squeeze on her hand. 'Yes, little darling?'

'I long to be kissed by you again,' finished a furiously blushing Anna.

'None but yourself stands between you and your desires, *lapooshka*.'

Nervously, she lifted her head. She felt herself melt beneath his eyes. His mysterious, enchanting beauty was so close. Too close. The breath of his softly parted lips alighted tenderly onto her own longing lips.

She closed her eyes and leaned forward. She stopped when her lips brushed against his. Their warm softness spread a burning, heavenly ache pulsing through her.

'Sasha, kiss me...'

'No.'

The ache deepened under the caress of his hot breath. 'Kiss me.'

'Take that ring off your finger and toss it into river, and I will do anything that you desire.'

The longing was unbearable. She lifted her head, opened her eyes and looked down at the ring encircling her ring finger. It was silver set with a large diamond. She felt no fondness for it, and for herself could happily have tossed the thing away. She had wanted a beautiful blue sapphire, not a wretched cold, colourless diamond. It had always been a painful reminder of her disappointed hopes. Hopes that had once been so high.

Then she looked back at the man calmly gazing at her. Every line and curve of his face was heavenly poetry, and its every look and stirring divine music. She longed to become intimately acquainted with its every rapturously beautiful nuance. To unveil the mystery of its heavenly secrets and unite her spirit with his forever.

She fingered the shackle of her bondage. 'What if I just take it off? Will you kiss me then?'

'No.'

She yielded to the pull of her heart and leaned forward once more. 'Kiss me, I'm begging you.'

'No.'

'Why not?'

'Because those lips, they belong to another. What is black cannot be white also.'

Nothing reached her senses except the sound of his burnished voice and the throbbing pulse of the warm blood passing through the velvet lips her mouth brushed against. 'Some thieves are welcome...' she whispered.

'Throw away the ring first.'

She was wrecked with the torture of being so close to the thing her heart begged for. 'Stop being so honourable and just kiss me!'

'No.'

'Oh damn you, Sasha Ivanovsky!' she cried in wretched frustration. 'I hate you! I was never so miserable until I met you—I wish I'd never met you!' Then she jumped to her feet and stormed off.

10

I Remember the Charming Sound of the Waltz

A MUSICAL evening. Anna took another gulp of claret. A musical evening with guests. She emptied her glass down her throat. A musical evening where she was expected to sing. Anna put the claret decanter to her lips and just swallowed. Then she fixed a china-doll smile firmly on her lips and entered the parlour, where the setting sun's last golden rays flooded it with warmth.

The first person Anna's eyes tripped over was Ivanovsky. He was seated in the window seat of the far-side bay window. Sitting on either side of him like roosting birds were Mabel and Mandy. Mabel appeared to be showing him a drawing.

Anna's eyes recovered and roved on. Jennifer's husband sat in *his* leather armchair reading the newspaper. As usual, he did not seem remotely interested in the rest of the room's occupants. Social gatherings, especially musical ones, bored him. Come to think of it, anything not concerned with business, finance or sport bored him. Jennifer and Mrs Dean stood near the grand fireplace, conversing quietly over a cup of tea, and Mr Sleighman sat at the grand piano riffling through some sheet music while Millie Dean stood beside him chattering and giggling.

Anna silently shook her head. Silly girl. There may be very few men about in such a small settlement, but young girls still ought to maintain standards and not throw themselves at any youngish man. Although Mr Sleighman did not appear to mind being thrown at. He was chattering quite as much as she.

Mr Sleighman caught sight of Anna. 'Hello, how're you?' he said in his usual quiet, breathy tones, nervously getting up and padding over.

'I am well, Mr Sleighman.'

He hesitantly took her hand and kissed it. 'Nice to see you.'

She had never loved gloves more. This thick black pair was quite marvellous. She merely smiled weakly in response.

He shifted from foot to foot. 'That new beige dress you're wearing is nice.'

There was a tiny tightening of her lips. The dress was pink. Moreover, it was not new. 'Thank you.'

He flashed her a nervous smile. 'I can't wait for you to sing. You're very good at it.'

She took a nearby wineglass and poured its contents down her throat. 'Thank you.'

'So, did you have a good day?'

'It was tolerable, thank you.'

'Finally you are here!' cried Jennifer as she swept up beside Anna. 'So,' she said, gesturing to a new painting hanging on the wall, 'was it not kind of Mr Ivanovsky to gift us this marvellous painting?'

Anna was a little annoyed with herself for not having noticed it yet. 'Oh yes, certainly.'

The painting was a misty view of a sunrise. At first glance, it seemed vague and somewhat messy to her. But closer inspection drew a warmer response. The misty, ethereal shapes and blended, borderless colours seemed to be moving before her very eyes. It seemed as though the colours and forms united themselves with something inside of her and drew her into their soft, beautiful, ever-moving world.

'It is wonderful. These colours and forms are so warm, so alive,' said Anna.

'Yes, it's nice,' Mr Sleighman said flatly. 'But all of this emotional gushing about art doesn't come naturally to men. Women are much better at emotional, feeling things.'

She glanced down her nose at him. 'If that is indeed the case, I beg you to enlighten me as to why so many renowned artists are men?'

'Well, I—I—it's true that there're a lot of male artists...' Then he faded, lost for an answer.

There was more than a touch of unkindness in the look she bestowed on him. 'Indeed, Mr Sleighman.'

'It pleases you?'

Anna turned to find Ivanovsky smiling down on her. 'Yes, I like it very much.'

'Good, I am very happy you are satisfied.'

She felt her cheeks grow warm. That was exactly the phrase he had used as she lay in his arms that memorable night.

Ivanovsky turned to Mr Sleighman. '*Il fait très chaud.* Here this is usual for the time of year?'

Anna cringed with shame as Mr Sleighman looked blankly at the Russian. Her fiancé could not speak a word of French. The silence was deafening.

'Yes, this heat is usual for the time of year,' Anna replied at last, with an uncomfortable laugh.

Ivanovsky smiled apologetically as comprehension dawned. 'Ah, pardon me for taking liberty of assuming everyone can understand French. In Russia, French is terribly fashionable. Everyone wishing to appear civilised sprinkles their conversation with generous seasoning of it. I am afraid this frightful habit has not yet left me.'

The warmly graceful apology was faultless, but Mr Sleighman still shifted nervously from foot to foot, and did not answer with anything except a nervous grimace.

Ivanovsky glanced down at the book Anna was unthinkingly clutching. 'I have always thought Pushkin's *Eugene Onegin* a great work. Is this your first time reading it?'

'Yes,' Anna replied with the slight fluster of someone caught doing a thing they did not really wish to be.

The book had been bequeathed to her by Miss Dora Bingham,

who was unspeakably thrilled by Anna's unexpected joining of the ranks of wild romantics. Not that she had joined them of course, Anna told herself. Everyone in Auckland had merely decided that she had.

'You are enjoying it?'

She felt like a fresh-faced schoolgirl as she bashfully met Ivanovsky's gaze. 'Yes, it is most interesting.'

Ivanovsky looked at the shortest member of the group. 'Do you like to read, Mr Sleighman?'

The reverend gave a peeved jerk of the head. 'Most books contain a load of rubbish. I prefer to learn from the book of life.'

Ivanovsky looked unruffled and deeply interested. 'What is this rubbish that you refer to?'

'Many books contain corrupting, subversive ideas. These books contradict the word of God and are filled with vile, sinful filth. Weaker readers such as children and females may be led into sin and error by books. Many books should be burnt.'

Ivanovsky replied to Mr Sleighman's outburst with a polite inclination of the head and a pained smile.

Anna knew what he was thinking. The book of life is often very thin, and enclosing one's faith in a wall of ignorance is no path to take. Yet his tolerance for Mr Sleighman's views clearly went as far as keen interest, and his calm politeness provided ample evidence that he upheld Mr Sleighman's right to have and express such opinions. Anna could not help being as impressed with Ivanovsky as she was ashamed of her fiancé.

'So,' said Jennifer, 'now that everyone is here, I think we can begin. Perhaps, Mr Sleighman, you and Miss Dean might like to provide our opening scene?'

Soon Mr Sleighman was seated at the piano while Millie Dean stood beside it. After a quick nod from Millie, Mr Sleighman began. The song was *Blow the Wind Southerly*, and Millie made a fine job of it. Although not spectacular, her soprano voice was natural, light and pretty in tone.

Anna refilled her wineglass again. Millie was a much better singer than she was. When a girl from a remote settlement who is almost twelve years younger than you is that much better than you are, thought an anxious Anna, then you ought not to display the fact. Millie Dean always showed Anna up on such occasions.

Anna hated such occasions. She drained her glass again.

When the song was finished, Millie bowed like a dewy-petaled rose bobbing in a morning breeze. Her large, heavy-lashed eyes shone brightly with girlish pleasure at the enthusiastic applause of Mr Sleighman and the other seated guests. Anna applauded just as enthusiastically as the other listeners did. Millie was a delightful singer, and it was not her fault if Anna lagged far behind her in the vocal stakes. Anna bore no resentment.

As soon as Millie had retired to a seat, Mabel leapt up. 'Play *Humpty Dumpty*, Mr Sleighman!'

'Yeah, we want to sing *Humpty Dumpty*!' cried Mandy, jumping up too.

'Girls, girls!' urged their red-faced mother. 'Do let the grown-ups alone. They do not wish to play nursery rhymes!'

'No, do as your mother says,' said Mr Sleighman. 'I'm sure Anna would like to sing next.'

Anna reached for another glass of wine.

'But we want to do *Humpty Dumpty*!'

Mandy joined her twin in jumping up and down. 'Pleeease!'

Mr Sleighman looked annoyed as he fended the twins off with a music book. 'I'm really not sure I know that tune—and it's not suitable for a grown-up party!'

'Children, children, behave!' pleaded their shame-faced mother, wringing her hands helplessly.

'You *do* know it!' quipped Mabel.

'Yeah, just so!'

'*Excusé moi...*'

Along with everyone else in the room, Anna turned to see who had spoken. Looking rather amused, Ivanovsky sat calmly with his hand raised like a schoolboy in class. The ironic gesture was not lost on Mrs Dean. She went even redder.

'I would like to volunteer to play this tune for you.'

A cheer went up from the twins, and a moment later the laughing Ivanovsky was being led (or should that be pulled?) towards the piano by Mabel and Mandy.

'You have music for this?' he asked, once the twins had installed him at the piano.

'You do not know the tune to *Humpty Dumpty*?' gasped Mandy, her eyes wide in surprise.

'No Mandushka, I do not. In Russia, we do not have this tune.'

Mabel seized the pile of sheet music sitting atop the piano. 'Let me look—'

'No, it's here, it's here!' cried Mandy, waving the book above her head.

Ivanovsky covered his ears with his hands in mock-pain. 'Owww…'

'Sorry,' giggled Mabel. 'We're like a pair of quacking ducks. You told us.'

'Yeah, just so,' added a giggling Mandy.

Ivanovsky smiled at the twins. 'So, you are ready?'

They nodded, and he began. In perfect sync, Mabel and Mandy acted out sitting on a wall as they sang the words. Then with the words 'had a great fall', they fell to the ground in a heap, after which they acted out desperately trying to put each other back together again. The over-blown looks of mock-misery they wore as they sat on the floor after failing to put 'Humpty together again' were so droll that everyone was in stitches. Anna laughed so hard she almost spilt her wine, and even Mrs Dean laughed a little.

Ivanovsky got up from the piano and knelt behind the twins. A moment later an arm was around each laughing, shrieking twin and he had lifted them up. The girls were then deposited onto the sofa. 'There, you are happy now?'

'Yes, yes, yes!'

'Sasha, you are the best!'

'Totally, just so!' cried Mandy, planting a kiss on his cheek.

After that, Mrs Dean appeared to decide that everyone could do with a little calmness. She sat down at the piano and began a very respectable rendition of Beethoven's *Moonlight Sonata*.

Anna's brother-in-law returned to his paper, but all the other audience members listened attentively as the calm, reflective notes rolled ponderously around the large parlour. The wood-panelled ceiling provided an excellent acoustic.

Anna's eyes wandered too. Upon encountering Sasha Ivanovsky, they came to rest. He was seated across the other side of the semi-circle of chairs from her, with Mabel on one side and Mandy on the other. She admired the effect of the soft pink light falling onto his face as he gazed contemplatively out of the window.

But before she had time to look away, his drowsy-lidded brown eyes met hers. He smiled gently and inclined his head slightly.

Feeling her cheeks grow warm, Anna stuffed her ring-bearing hand down the side of the chair and lowered her eyes. She felt a little betrayed to discover that her lips had lifted into a shy smile. There was something about that Russian which left one so terribly exposed.

She frowned in annoyance and took another sip of wine. Being unable to look a gentleman in the eye without blushing like a schoolgirl. Such weakness. She really was going soft in the head. Next thing she would be mooning around reading poetry like Miss Dora.

Once Mrs Dean had finished the piece, Jennifer declared an adjournment for supper. While everyone else clustered around the buffet, Anna remained seated. She was not hungry.

A plate of lobster salad suddenly appeared before her. She looked up to see who held it out. It was Ivanovsky.

'Miss Anna, you must eat something.'

She looked down again. 'Thank you, but I really do not have any appetite.'

A moment later he was seated beside her on the sofa, with a concerned frown upon his face. 'Eat it anyway, it will do you good.'

She shook her head distastefully. 'No, I assure you, I cannot manage a thing.'

He leaned in close. 'Anna, if you do not get some food down there to soak up that alcohol, you will regret it.'

She stiffened with mortification and stared fixedly at her knees. How dare he.

The plate was placed on her lap, and she felt her fingers being manually closed around a fork. 'Eat.'

'I will try,' she faltered, 'But I really am feeling a little indisposed.'

'That is hardly surprising. Anyone with that much strong drink down them would be a little indisposed, to say the least,' came his hushed yet insistent whisper.

She stabbed angrily at the lobster with her fork. The knowledge that Ivanovsky did not drink made the situation especially humiliating. The way members of her acquaintance who were involved with the temperance movement looked disapprovingly at the Browns really raised her ire. Anna could not stand anyone being more respectable than she was.

Picking at the food even more reluctantly than she usually did, she reached for her wineglass in order to wash the food down her parched throat.

But a masculine hand covered the glass. 'No, you have had enough.'

A spark of temper flashed to life within, and she was about to let loose the retort burning on the tip of her tongue. But as suddenly as it flared up, it was gone. She *was* slightly drunk. There was no point trying to deny it. Letting out a painfully reluctant sigh of defeat, she sulkily went back to stabbing at the lobster salad.

Once supper was over, Anna's worst nightmare came true.

'Everyone has waited long enough, Miss Anna. You must sing now,' declared Mr Sleighman.

Putting on her most pitiful expression, Anna felt her brow with a droopingly feeble hand. 'Pray, might I be excused just this once? I really am feeling awfully tired, and my poor head aches terribly.'

'N, you absolutely must not disappoint your poor fiancé,' Jennifer said firmly, shunting Anna along towards the piano, where Mr Sleighman sat waiting.

'Hearing you sing *Casta Diva* is a real treat,' Mr Sleighman extorted eagerly.

Anna could have sobbed.

'Oh yes, you simply must,' said Jennifer, wearing her most no-nonsense air.

A tiny whimper escaped Anna as she found the score thrust into her shaking hands. *Casta Diva* from Bellini's opera *Norma* was a terribly demanding aria. The notes jumped around on the page in vigorous abandon, and to her, it seemed as though they were gleefully taunting her like spiteful children. Anna's voice could reach some spectacular high notes, which was why everyone pushed her to sing it. But when it soared up to great heights, her voice developed a wobble like a loose wheel on a speeding cart that was about to come spinning off at any moment.

'No, not *Casta Diva*,' she pleaded weakly.

'It is *such* a treat,' said Jennifer.

'But I would rather sing *The Ash Grove*—'

'I prefer *Casta Diva*,' said Mr Sleighman, and without waiting for an answer from Anna, started to play the opening bars of *Casta Diva*.

Anna took a final gulp from the wineglass resting atop the piano and began. As she laboured through note after excruciating note, Anna felt as though her body's every last fibre was a metal spring stretched to breaking point. Approaching the aria's high notes was an especially rarefied terror. As she climbed them, her voice started to wobble like a bicycle with a bent wheel, and cracks worthy of an earthquake-stricken wall opened up. It felt as though the music was torturing her entire body from the inside out. She let out a sigh of relief as the last tortuous notes died away.

Mr Sleighman's applause was loudest of all. 'Bravo! bravo!' he cried, getting to his feet.

With an apologetic smile of pure pain on her face, Anna slunk away with her head hanging.

'Encore, encore!' cried Mr Sleighman.

Anna set down the wineglass she had just drained and shook her head. 'No really, I could not possibly hog the floor any longer.'

Mr Sleighman held up a music book. 'But this Rossini aria you sing so well—'

'No, no, no!' she fired back rapidly, making for the door leading out onto the veranda with a wine bottle in her hand. 'I must take the air for a minute.'

Mr Sleighman planted a restraining hand on the door. 'But you sing it so well!'

Anna took Mr Sleighman's words not as a compliment but as a symptom of his tone-deafness and lack of musical taste. Moreover, she was sure that his enthusiasm about her performing had more than a little to do with the opportunity it gave him to display his own skills. Although she herself felt that his piano playing lacked all true artistic feeling, merely being mechanical in its skilled performance.

Her neck felt as though a tight wire encircled it. 'My throat is too tired—'

'Rubbish, you're just being a hypochondriac!' came his irritated response.

Jennifer nodded agreement. 'Yes, do stop being such a child. You are about to become a married woman, for goodness sake!'

As a result of being ganged up on in this way, the most humiliating, mortifying thing happened. A tear overflowed Anna's eye and slipped down her cheek. She stared back at the selfish, extorting faces. Her mind was a barren plain of horror.

Then Ivanovsky appeared at Anna's side. For once, she was glad of his sudden presence. 'Perhaps, Mr Sleighman, we gentlemen ought to be gallant and allow the ladies to rest and be serenaded by us?'

Anna could have sobbed with gratitude at the Russian's careful rescue.

Mr Sleighman eyed Ivanovsky like a terrier that has just found itself face-to-face with a tiger. 'Well, ahem, perhaps we could...but I'm sure Miss Anna would be generous enough to sing us just one more song...'

Anna felt Ivanovsky's hand touch her elbow lightly. 'Miss Anna, you desire to rest, do you not?'

Blinking furiously, she nodded.

With his gentle hand still holding her arm, Ivanovsky guided Anna towards a chair. Once she was seated, he smiled tenderly down at her. 'Mademoiselle, what do you wish me to sing for you?'

She could not help returning his smile with one of her own, although hers was much more uncertain and watery. 'Could you sing for me something from Russia?'

'It would be my pleasure—'

'But we don't know Russian,' Mr Sleighman interrupted, with a slight nastiness in his voice. 'We'll have no idea what you're singing about.'

'I will tell you what stories the songs speak of before I begin,' Ivanovsky answered, without taking his loving eyes off Anna.

'But I won't be able to accompany you,' whined Mr Sleighman.

Ivanovsky produced a guitar. 'I shall accompany myself.'

Anna told herself off for not noticing that the instrument had been leaning against the wall near the piano all that time. It must have been his, as she had never seen it before.

Mr Sleighman had one more shot. 'But the guitar doesn't sound good in a large room like this. The piano is much better.'

If Ivanovsky heard this, he did not show it. He busied himself tuning the guitar at the piano, after which he drew the piano stool out and sat down with the guitar resting on his knee.

'The first song I would like to sing is called *I remember the charming sound of the waltz*. A charming, languid, glorious waltz sung on a spring night by an unknown voice is remembered. The memories are recalled in dark winter, while a blizzard howls beneath the wind and no sounds of the waltz are heard. "Where is that glorious waltz?" the voice ends by asking.'

Anna felt as though an arrow had pierced through her and pinned her to the back of her chair. The song, with its slow, simple waltz rhythm and fragile bitter-sweetness, she knew was just for her. He sought to remind her of *that* night. She listened to the song's reflective, quietly wonder-filled melody with utter fixation. Whether in horror or happiness she was not sure.

Ivanovsky was utterly immersed in the music. It seemed to fill his body and soul completely, and the deep sensitivity and emotion his voice, facial expression and gesture expressed were profoundly moving.

Ivanovsky modestly acknowledged the warm applause which greeted the song's end. 'Next I would like to sing for you *Do Not Awaken Memories.* "Do not awaken memories of days gone by, you shall not reawaken past desires in my soul", begs the voice. "Your daring gaze towards me do not direct, with wondrous thoughts of love beguile me not." The final couplet says: "of happiness only once in this life do we partake, warmed by the sacred fire of love we are revived".'

Anna hardly dared to breathe. Those words could have been her own. *She* did not wish him to awaken memories, *she* was determined he would not awaken past desires, *she* did not wish him to direct his daring gaze upon her as he was doing now.

His eyes rested powerfully on her, their soulful depths holding her heart enthralled. She was desperate to look away, but she could not free her eyes from his smoulderingly melancholy, quietly passionate gaze. Wondrous thoughts of love utterly beguiled her as the enchanting melody swept all things along with its slow rise and fall.

So terrifyingly enthralled was Anna that she forgot to applaud along with everyone else when the song's last hushed tones faded. Her fingers dug sharply into the chair's arms as she waited for the next song.

The slight shyness in his warm smile as he bowed modestly in reply to the applause made her heart melt within her.

He sat back down. 'Thank you. This next song is a traditional Russian crying song. It is called *Oh, if Only I Could Express in Words*. It says "oh, if only I could express the full depth of my suffering in words, the voice of doubt in your soul would be silenced, and then I could rest, dear one. But if you were to hear this hidden sound, your heart would be shattered".'

The song's slow, simple beginning slid into a deeper, rocking rhythm, then the voice rose to passionate, agonised heights that finished with drawn out notes sounding a cry of pure, deep agony that seemed to come directly from his heart. And that cry found its echo in Anna's own heart.

She covered her mouth with her hands as her breath caught painfully in her throat. Her heart burned with his hurt, and with her own hurt. How blind she had been not to see that, from that moment Ivanovsky had stepped out into the moonlight, no possibility of happiness existed for her other than in his arms. No woman who had known such love could ever be free of its shadow.

And it was such love as lasted for an eternity. He would never stop suffering, and neither would she.

The moment the keen applause had died down sufficiently for her not to appear impolite, Anna hurried for the door leading outside. A terrible, sickening fear gripped her. To have been cursed so by fate.

In the close darkness, she gasped with agony and stumbled into the garden, her hands still clutched to her mouth to stifle the sobs filling her throat. She came to rest on the seat in the herb garden, and sat there shaking with unspoken grief.

'Anya, I am so sorry.'

'No, I cannot speak to you, cannot see you!—' She covered her face and turned away from the shadowy figure standing before her. But his scent reached her senses even though she sought to block him from them.

He dropped to his knees before her and clasped her hand. 'Come with me! Dare to venture out into the unknown!'

She shook her head abruptly, the mere thought of the unknown making her heart race with fear. 'No, I cannot! I am too weak, too afraid—'

'*Mllaya moyna*, I know I am lowly painter who cannot offer you worldly riches or prestige. Instead, I offer you my undying love and devotion always. If you come with me I will never abandon you, and I will give you everything I can.'

The simple, quietly spoken words were filled with love. But to part of her they were abominable. The threshold he would draw her across gaped before her in all its terror, and something shifted within her.

How could he torment her with illusions, with vague fantasies, how could he try to draw her away from a respectable match with a God-fearing man, how could he attempt to tear her from the bosom of her family? For that was what these wild romantic notions were: crazed delusions that contained nothing but ruin.

'Tell me you do not love me.'

Anna could not. Panic suddenly possessed her. She turned on him in a flash and threw the contents of her wineglass in his face. 'No! Go away!'

The look on his gentle, thoughtful face was the worst sight her eyes had ever seen. Pain and deep sadness filled it. But far worse was the love residing there unchanged. His sad brown eyes rested calmly on her as he brought a handkerchief up to his wine-dripping face.

The red wine stain would never come out of his white silk cravat. That was the strange thought passing through Anna's mind as she regarded him with fear and horror.

His look did not change as he slowly rose. Then he cast a final look of profound sadness on her before fading into the night.

No clear thought or feeling passed through Anna as she walked along the hard, sandy path leading down to the seashore in the darkness. Her usual seat on the beached log provided welcome rest.

But the sea's usually beguiling voice did not welcome her. Instead the listless waves lapped insipidly, seethed broodingly, spat poisonously and frothed hissingly. The sea's sickened rhythm was deathly, quietly filled with a rage that would not speak its name. It did not need to. Anna knew why it was angry. It was angry because she had rejected its gift. Rejected its gift of love. Its gift of life.

Choking with tears, she turned from the ocean's once-welcoming face and ran. The sea did not forgive those who scornfully returned its offerings. It did not forgive.

Seized by an unspeakable terror, she did not stop running until she reached the veranda of Gravemore House. There, she found an almost full wine bottle and retreated back into the garden.

The seat in the herb garden had been the scene of two shattering encounters with Ivanovsky. Anna wanted to sit there and nowhere else.

The shadows grew blacker and blacker, and still Anna set there. Then the stars appeared in the night sky. Holding the now half-empty wine bottle, Anna stared fixedly up at them. When a crescent moon joined her celestial sisters, the watching woman's eyes had barely moved once.

Not long after the bottle's final drops had slid down her throat, Anna passed out on the garden seat in a drunken stupor.

* * * *

There was no ticking clock in the herb garden. Neither was there a fluffy feather pillow. Anna's consciousness rose a little closer to the surface. She haltingly moved her hand out. It met the cold, hard resistance of an iron bed-frame.

Blinking furiously at the painful daylight, she slowly prised her reluctant eyelids open. Yes, there was no doubting it. She was lying in her bed, in her bedroom. And—she looked down to check—she was not wearing her dress any longer. Just her shift.

This was all well and good in itself. However, there was one little problem: she could not remember how she had got there. Had Ivanovsky returned? She pushed the thought from her mind. But the option that replaced it was even worse. What if it had been Jennifer?

Anna groaned aloud and clutched a hand to her throbbing head. Her mouth felt like a sand-filled desert and her stomach like a swamp. What if she still felt like this by two O'clock? She would just have to get married feeling like that.

A knock sounded on the door, and a maid bustled in.

As Molly set about opening the curtains, Jennifer entered. 'Time to get up, N. It will take the remaining four hours left to us to get you ready for the wedding.'

Anna was forced to shut her eyes against the glaring daylight.

'The Dean girls will be arriving in about half an hour to help you dress,' continued Jennifer, 'and to get themselves dressed in their bridesmaids' outfits.'

As soon as she was alone once more, Anna gave in to the tide of nausea that had slowly been rising since she awoke, and dashed to the window.

Having emptied some of the previous night's excess into the hydrangeas below, she looked up to find a change in the usual view out over the sea. A small ship anchored in the bay formed a ghostly presence as it loomed out of the mists hanging over the grey ocean. The coastal ship *Fearless One* had at last come to pick up the wool. It was awaiting the high tide at one O'clock, when the boisterous breakers would fall still and the wool bales could be transferred from the horse drawn wagons that would bring them down to the sea and onto a rowing boat that would ferry them out to be hoisted aboard the ship.

Ivanovsky would be leaving with the wool bales. This was good. No more would his presence beguile her. No more would wild, wondrous thoughts of love torment her. She would once more be sensible, cucumber-cool Anna. Then, at last, she would be able to rest in peace.

The thought that her torment might simply increase in his absence presented itself to her, but she quickly bludgeoned it to death. No, when he went, the torment would go with him.

Soon the twins burst into the room, followed a dignified few minutes later by Millie. Although Mabel and Mandy were supposed to be there to help Anna ready herself, they merely helped a box of hairpins fall onto the floor, a vase of flowers fall over on the table, and a kitten unravel two spools of thread and a length of ribbon. All the while making a din loud enough to shake any lurking woodworm clean out of the furniture.

Millie proved a much greater help, and it was not long before Anna's hair was beginning to look quite comely. However, as Millie worked, her usual giggly chatter was entirely absent. Anna wondered what on earth was the matter with her. But the mystery was solved when Anna silently returned from a tea-scavenging mission downstairs.

'It was so horrid,' Millie's voice reached Anna as she paused before the ajar door. 'I was standing out at the far end of the veranda when—when he just came up close and—and started putting these wet kisses on me and licking my ear!'

'Argh!'

'Vile rat!'

'Totally, just so!'

'I said no, but—but he just kept on!'

'Argh, how revolting!'

'Yeah, that's vastly disgusting.'

'I know I had been talking to him and such, but I did not mean anything by it.'

'Yeah, but you were vastly asking for it giggling over him all enthuzimuzzy all the time.'

'Totally, just so. Vastly asking for it.'

'Yeah, anyone with half a brain could have seen that doing that was all-over red.'

'I do not know why I am speaking of this to you brats; all you do is be horrid!'

'You don't know much—'

'Shut your cake-hole, Mabel. Millie is right; we *are* being rather horrid.'

'Yeah. The one we ought to be moaning about is that hugger-mugger cheater.'

'Totally. He is a vile dog!'

'I never want to see him again!' came Millie's tearful voice.

'Don't worry, chuckaboo; us two will find a way of getting even with the animal!'

'Just so! We'll get the low worm.'

'Yeah, we won't shoot into the brown.'

'Yeah, we'll not fail. The nasty gal-sneaker had better look out.'

On that ominous note, Anna silently retreated back to the top of the stairs, from whence she advanced once again. This time she hummed a tune as she went along. Suddenly she realised the tune was *I Remember the Charming Sound of the Waltz*. She instantly stopped humming. Good God.

* * * *

By now, Anna's dark brown locks had been combed, teased and pinned into an impressive up-do decorated with white silk flowers. As the bridesmaids now needed to get themselves ready, Anna left them with the fortifying tea and swept back down the stairs, meaning to get a little air.

Her own corset was already tightly laced in to a trim twenty-one inches. She had never achieved this gratifying number before, but it had only been managed with a combination of a bed-frame for her to hold onto and Millie hauling back on the laces with all her might. All the petticoats and padded rolls which were needed to provide the foundations for her wedding dress were also in place. Anna had just thrown a loose housedress over it all until she was ready to put on her wedding dress.

She passed through the back door and wandered across the lawn. The ground was damp with rain that had merely been enough to make the sky dull grey and the earth's surface drearily soggy, but not to provide the browning grasses with any useful moisture. The light drizzle had blown in with an unseasonably cold southerly weather front.

Although she hugged her arms tightly against the bitingly cold wind, the chill soon forced Anna to retreat back towards the house. As she neared the wisteria-covered trellis screening the walkway leading to the door, the sound of booted footsteps reached her ears.

Fearing it was Ivanovsky, she was in amongst the concealing branches of a large lilac tree growing near the trellis in a flash. She had resolved not to speak to him ever again. He was nothing but trouble. She had never committed a shameful act until he appeared. Guilt stilled stabbed at her over the unspeakable rudeness with the wine glass.

She could see Ivanovsky standing near the back door. His warm, travel-ready clothing had the usual unmistakable touch of foreignness and unsettling bohemian air about it. His smart frockcoat, with its velvet collar and cuffs, was a dusky shade of plum, and his black top hat was set on at a slightly rakish angle. But worst of all was the silk necktie. Rather than wearing a discrete tie or small, flat cravat fastened with a pin, he instead wore a voluminous pale gold necktie fastened in a floppy, generous bow. Adding the final touch of horrifying individuality was the richly patterned paisley scurf draped over his neck. The trunk she had rescued from the sea set on the ground nearby, and he paced slowly up and down the path as though waiting.

As he came nearer to her hiding place, she could hear him softly humming a melancholy melody to himself. He paused, took out a fob watch and flicked it open to check the time. He then slipped it back and resumed pacing thoughtfully along the path.

As he turned for another length of the path, his hummed melody took flight as song. The song he sang to himself was a Russian song she had never heard before. Anna could not understand any of its words. However, when the song ended it began again in English.

You cannot understand my sadness,
When, ravaged by sorrow,
You did not come to see me off on a long journey

One who feels with his soul,
One who feels with his soul.
You cannot understand, you cannot understand,
You cannot understand my sadness.

You cannot understand my sadness,
Unless in eyes so dear to you,
You have read coldness
And beheld contempt in them

You cannot understand, you cannot understand,
You cannot understand my sadness.

So that was what the words meant. The guilt she had been attempting to strangle to death all morning rose up from its knees and bit into her heart. Sasha Ivanovsky had shown her nothing but love, respect and kindness. While she had thrown wine and insults into his face.

Ivanovsky picked up the trunk and slowly began walking down the path leading to the seashore. Anna watched intently as his receding figure travelled ever further from her.

But in place of the relief she had promised herself, she felt instead the teeth of regret sinking deeper into her with every onwards step Ivanovsky took. He had stolen her heart. And the only way she could ever be whole again was to unite her life with his. Forever.

When he reached the centre of the brown-grassed paddock, the pain became unbearable. To be wild, romantic and brave, to throw aside respectability and sacrifice everything for the man she loved—that was what she would do!

Anna broke into a run.

Forty paces from him she slowed to a walk and let the hem of her dress fall back to the ground. The rustle of her skirts and her panting breaths appeared to have alerted Ivanovsky to Anna's presence, for he slowed and turned towards her. He did not speak as she nervously drew near. In his expression, she read only patient composure.

Hard as it was to look her shame in the face, she forced her eyes to hold his gaze as she haltingly approached. 'Sasha...'

'Yes, Anya?'

She flinched before his solemn, penetrating gaze. 'I...' But her voice faded along with her resolve.

She could not do it. Could not say those words which would sever her from her family and from wealth and respectability forever.

She pulled cold composure tightly about herself and held out the handkerchief embroidered with the initials A. I. which she had chanced upon behind her bedroom door. 'I—I merely wished to return this to you...'

He smiled sadly and politely tipped his hat, but said nothing. Then he took the thing she offered.

Although the love in his eyes was unchanged, Anna could sense that a veil had been drawn between her and him. He had withdrawn himself from her like...yes, like a mourner drawing back from a deceased loved one's cold corpse before it was placed in the grave.

The Russian stepped forward and lightly placed a kiss on her cold, clammy forehead. 'Goodbye, *doosha maya*.'

A tiny, frightened voice tried to struggle to the surface. 'Sasha, I—I wa...' But it died and sunk back into the murky depths.

The look he rested on her was filled with quiet hope. It willed her to say it. To say she would come.

The faint little voice deep within her screamed out for his love. It begged her pride to yield and her fear to flee. But she also wanted the large house, the large staff, the large wardrobe, the exalted position in society, the civilised, dignified life...

Shaking his head sadly, Ivanovsky turned and walked away.

Anna silently begged his receding figure to stop, to look back at her just one last time.

Ivanovsky did not so much as pause once. His eyes were fixed on the road ahead of him, and his onward step bold and unhesitating.

Her heart screamed with agony as the beguiling Russian finally disappeared behind the sand dunes. Now she stood all alone in the barren field of shrivelled grass beneath the miserable grey skies. A bitterly cold southerly wind moaned desolately as it hurried fretfully by, and the distant bleating of sheep sounded from the scarred hills.

Anna turned and ran for the house.

11

Farewell, Happiness

A BONE-CHILLING numbness enshrouded Anna as she stumbled back into the house. Her mind seemed frozen in that moment of his leaving. Upon reaching the front parlour, she rung the bell and sunk into the nearest chair.

Molly the maid appeared at the door a moment later. 'Yes, Miss Anna?'

'Tea. I need tea.'

Molly bobbed and hurried off towards the kitchen.

Anna stared fixedly into the distance as she waited. But instead of seeing the wall in front of her, she saw Ivanovsky's beloved figure striding alone into the wide blue yonder with never a backward glance. Not one.

When the cup of tea was in front of Anna and she was alone

once more, she glided over to the drinks stand and returned with a bottle of whisky. She shakily poured a large measure into the tea and sat back down. When she lifted the cup and saucer, her hands shivered and trembled so violently that hot tea overflowed the rattling cup and dribbled into the bouncing saucer.

She managed to gulp a few mouthfuls without spilling tea everywhere, then set the saucer back down and stared vacantly out the window. No more did the bright waters dance with the laughing sunbeams. No more did the waves whisper of wondrous dreams and faraway shores. Today the flat grey waters just lay there dully, and the waves flopped tiredly onto the beach.

'Are you listening to me?'

Anna suddenly realised that someone was speaking. She refocused her eyes and found Jennifer's sourly frowning face glaring down at her.

'Answer me when I talk to you!'

'Pardon me, I was lost in thought,' Anna replied emotionlessly, not looking at her sister.

'Look at the state of your hair!' Looking like she may well be at the end of her tether, Jennifer threw her hands into the air. 'Now all this will have to be put back in order. We will never get to the church on time!'

'I do not care if we are late,' Anna said flatly. 'Mr Sleighman can wait.'

'What has got into you? I hope God will forgive you for your unkindness to poor Mr Sleighman, for I am not sure I shall!'

'If Mr Sleighman is poor it is because he has made himself so.'

Jennifer seized hold of her sister's arm. 'Anna, stop this nonsense at once!'

Anna did not put up any resistance. She allowed Jennifer to pull her up and start dragging her towards the door.

'Talk about a difficult bride; I have never in my life come across such moody impossibility!' continued the younger sister. 'Anyone would think you do not wish to get married at all today!'

'I do not give a toss whether I get married to Mr Sleighman today or not. I do not care if I ever get married. I do not care if I live or if I die.'

Once the utterly frazzled, almost speechlessly horrified Jennifer had hauled her glassy-faced sister upstairs, she thrust her back into the bedroom. 'Millie, sort this mess out!'

Floral bouquets, wedding clothes and feminine accessories of every description littered the room. In the midst of all this stood Millie, taking tissue paper-wrapped shoes out of a dainty box.

'Mabel, Mandy, come and put your shoes on,' she called to the twins, who sat on the bed surrounded by clothes.

'Nooo, I don't want to,' Mabel whined tearfully.

'Yeah, don't w-want to,' Mandy added with a sob.

'You know you cannot go down to see Sasha off on the boat. Now come and put your shoes on.'

'Why n-not?'

'Because you will get your dresses all dirty, and because there is no time if we are to arrive at the wedding on time.'

Rubbing their wet eyes and dragging their feet, the twins mournfully obeyed. Millie quickly turned her attention onto the bride, who was soon sitting before the dressing table while her drooping brown locks were skillfully coaxed back into place.

There was a knock on the door, and a rosy face topped by a frilly little cap popped around the door. 'I found this here note sitting on the hall table, and with it this roll of paper.'

'Who is it addressed to?' Millie asked through a mouthful of hairpins.

'The note says "to Mabya and Manduska", and the scroll has written on it "A Russian artist's response to just criticism".'

'Give it here, give it here!' cried the twins, rushing to claim their prize.

When the twins had mugged her of the note, Molly the maid came over and placed the scroll on the dressing table. 'Don't know who it's for. Perhaps you'd like to see to it, Miss Anna.'

'It's a puzzle!' Mandy's shriek hit Anna's ears from across the room.

'Yeah, it's a clue!'

'It says: "Where the thing of mouse's dreams is bound, there will another question be found." '

'Oh woe, that is so hard!'

'Totally, Sasha is vastly clever!'

'Let's think, let's think!'

'Yeah, what is the thing of mouse's dreams?'

'What about a cat?'

'But that would be a nightmare!'

'Yeah, but that is a sort of dream!'

'Totally! What about a *mouse* trap?'

'Could be, but where is a mousetrap bound?'

'Yeah, just so…'

'I know, I know!' screamed Mabel, jumping up and down with excitement. 'It's cheese, it's cheese!'

Mandy started jumping too. 'Totally, it's got to be cheese!'

'Where is cheese bound?'

'Hmmm…'

'Let's think…'

'You know, I think I might have an idea…' mused Molly, pausing a thoughtful little finger on her lip.

Two shining rosy faces were turned on her in an instant. 'Yeah?'

'What about…the *cellar*? There's cheese in there bound in cloths and dippings of wax.'

'Yeah, that's it!' shrieked the twins in unison, stampeding out the door.

At first, Anna stared at the scroll like someone eyeing a thing the cat has dragged in. It was meant for her, of course. It was certainly a painting or drawing of some nature, and the irony of the words written on it were not lost on her. This was a tongue-in-cheek reference to her criticism of his portrait of her.

When Millie left the room on a hunting expedition that had hair ribbon as its quarry, Anna at last picked the scroll up. Wearing the expression of one opening a package of fish which may or may not have gone bad, she slowly pulled the ribbon tied around it undone.

Her guess proved right. It was indeed another portrait of her.

Pressing its curling edges down on the table, Anna stared grimly at the painting. She could not resist a black smile. This portrait was entirely opposite to the first one. She was depicted sitting on a half-open tomb amongst the other tombstones clustered in the graveyard. She was attired in a flowing gown of black, and rested her drooping head in a bony, almost transparently pale hand as she stared bleakly into space. A wilted, browning rose was held limply in her other hand. The eyes were glassy, the skin a pale, ashen shade that spoke of decay, and upon the downward-sagging lips rested the kiss of death. The mournful figure sat on the edge of the tomb as though waiting for the moment when death came to claim her and at last she could climb into her readied tomb and sleep the sleep of death.

The cold already gripping Anna tightened its icy hold. What did he mean by such a grisly offering? How could he play such a horrid joke on her? It was so cruel and false. She did not look like that—did she? Anna lifted her eyes up to the mirror.

While the pale face that looked dully back at her did not quite have the same deathly air as the one below it, the promise of decay lived in the blank eyes and depressed skin. A few more years of wretched sorrow, opium-imbibing and despair, and the portrait would not lie. Anna sprung up with a gasp, opened the drawer of the dressing table and dropped in the painting as though it was a vile horror.

Then she slammed the drawer shut. How could he do such a thing. How could he. So mean. So horrid. So insulting.

'Millie, where are you?' she cried. 'We are going to be late!'

* * * *

Anna almost fell on her face as she stepped out of the carriage.

'Accursed wedding dress!' she muttered savagely, hoicking its long train out from under her feet yet again.

Anna waited beside the carriage while her bridesmaids hurried about her putting the train and veil in order.

Once all was in place, Millie, as chief bridesmaid, gave the nod for the music to begin. The wedding march sounded forth from the church's tiny harmonium.

The bride received its pip-squeak sized tones contemptuously. Why could she not have a proper Auckland wedding? The great organ there would blast this little runt into the dust. Mr Sleighman had not been able to get leave to have two weeks off to travel up to Auckland. However, Anna did not see this as an acceptable excuse for such a low-class wedding. He should have wheedled it out of the bishop. The bishop was his own father, for God's sake! If a man could not even manage that, his wheedling technique really needed a brush-up.

The look the bride gave the front of the little wooden church was no more flattering than the one the organ had received. Its plain, humble face found no favour with her.

'Ready, my dear?'

She looked at her father. He was a tall man of austere appearance with king-sized sideburns. To his daughter it was like looking at a stranger. The time she had been away had made her realise that she hardly knew her father at all. They had never had an intimate conversation.

Anna nodded vaguely and slipped her hand under the arm he

offered.

She felt unusually breathless as she walked up the aisle, and her vision was very queer indeed. Everything she looked at seemed as though it was a reflection viewed in a shattered mirror. She hardly saw the people packed into the pews she passed on her way to the altar. Imbibing large quantities of wine and opium really did one no good at all.

She looked neither left nor right as she stood before the altar; her eyes were fixed instead on the simple wooden crucifix hanging above it. The interior of the church always seemed so bare, so hard, so cold. Much like the hearts of the people filling it. Anna did not know where God was to be found, but it certainly was not here.

'Dearly beloved, we are gathered here in the sight of God to join together this man and this woman in holy matrimony, which is an honourable estate,' the vicar's droning voice finally broke into her cold, still world, 'instituted of God in the time of man's innocency, signifying unto us the mystical union that is betwixt Christ and his church; which holy estate Christ adorned and beautified with his presence, and first miracle that he wrought; in Cana of Galilee; and is commended of Saint Paul to be honourable among all men: and therefore is not by any to be enterprised, nor taken in hand unadvisedly, lightly or wantonly to satisfy men's carnal lusts and appetites like brute beasts that have no understanding, but reverently, discreetly, advisedly, soberly, and in fear of God; duly considering the cause for which Matrimony was ordained.'

Well, that was this marriage condemned then, Anna thought grimly. For she was entering into it unadvisedly, and he wantonly.

When the bride's attention returned to the vicar, he was up to the third article. 'It was ordained for the mutual society, help, and comfort that the one ought to have of the other, both in prosperity and adversity...'

The only help and comfort Mr Sleighman can provide me is to remove himself from my presence, Anna silently added to the vicar's words. And mutual society? Mutual misery was a more likely result.

The vicar droned out the required questions of whether those present knew of any just impediments to the marriage.

No one spoke. Anna's glassy stare became glassier still. She faced the altar like a condemned woman facing the executioner's block. A hot teardrop overflowed each eye and silently slid down the bride's cold white cheeks. She let them roll impeded by neither finger nor handkerchief.

No one else heeded these glistening drops of sorrow either. The bridegroom was busy shifting from foot to foot and fidgeting with something in his pocket, while the vicar read out the ceremony with all the feeling of a machine.

The vicar looked to Mr Sleighman. 'Norris Derek Sleighman, wilt thou have this woman to thy wedded wife, to live together after God's ordinance in the holy estate of Matrimony? Wilt thou love her, comfort her, honour, and keep her, in sickness and in health; and forsaking all others, keep thee only unto her, so long as ye both shall live?'

Mr Sleighman, with shoulders hunched and head hanging floorwards, nodded uncertainly. 'I will.'

The vicar threw a look at the silently weeping bride that saw little and took in less. 'Anna Sarah Brown, wilt thou have this man to thy wedded husband, to live together after God's ordinance in the holy estate of Matrimony? Wilt thou obey him and serve him, love, honour, and keep him, in sickness and in health; and forsaking all others, keep thee only unto him, so long as ye both shall live?'

Anna turned to her bridegroom and looked at him properly for the first time that day. His unsteady eyes only held her gaze for a moment before they faltered and looked down once he had given her a weak smile. Nervously shifting from foot to foot, he fidgeted with his hands.

Her eyes roamed over his face. The engorged bottom lip sent a shiver of distaste coursing through her.

A slight murmur ran through the audience at Anna's delay. Mr Sleighman darted a nervous glance at her while the vicar cleared his throat impatiently.

Then Sleighman licked his lips. This was a mistake. A vision of a slimy leech drooling in anticipation of a promised feast of blood rose before her horrified mind. That lip was like a grave-worm waiting to feast on a fresh corpse. It would pick every last bit of tender meat off until there was nothing but dry bones left. Pick away until she was nothing but cold, brittle bones.

When she moved her eyes up to the full horror of his thick, brutal nose, another vision hovered before her hazy eyes. A pale, deathly woman bore a baby in her arms. Weeping silently, she halted before a lolling hyena and placed the peacefully sleeping child before it. Quick as a flash, the foul beast seized the angelic baby and dragged it off while the infant's screams pierced the air.

Anna staggered and covered her gaping mouth with her hands. A child—what if she was carrying *his* child? A child that would grow into the image of its father and expose its mother's shame to all the world! And what a home to descend into; misery, hate, hopelessness. And such a man for a father. What child of hers would have any chance?

Anna put a steadying hand on the nearby chair, and breathed deep. Drunk. That was what she was. Still drunk. She took another deep breath, and looked up again.

It was not him! Agonising grief suddenly gripped her. It was not him. Anna felt like she was crying deep inside herself. Not him, but some other bridegroom. Not him... Tears, falling like raindrops down a window pane... That would forever be the veil she viewed this life through. A fool she had been, thinking that she could ever be happy with any other after the fateful encounter on that midsummer night. No. Those who crossed paths with such love must surrender or suffer. Divine gifts cannot be rejected.

'Will you have this man?' the vicar prompted impatiently.

'I will not!' Anna cried suddenly.

Then she shoved Mr Sleighman aside, turned on her heels, and ran.

12

Oh, There Are Many Roads

ANNA halted abruptly. From the vantage point offered by the knoll the little church sat on, she could see the ship *Fearless One* rocking gently as she floated just beyond the breakers. A shaft of sunlight that had broken through the watery grey clouds hovering above painted the vessel in soft tones of golden yellow, and sent a myriad of glittering reflections dancing across the rippling sea around her.

But the human activities that the golden gleam alighted on filled Anna with panic. The *Fearless One*'s crew hurried about on deck and scrambled up the rigging as they weighed anchor and prepared to set sail.

'Mabel!' screamed Anna, turning back towards the church doors.

But there was no need to shout. Anna found herself face-to-face with the two littlest bridesmaids. 'Yeah?' they chorused, their rosy-cheeked faces shining with glee.

'My trousseau, I need my trousseau! Where the hell is it?'

'It's just in the carriage!' Mabel called over her shoulder, running towards one of the carriages parked outside the church.

'Yeah, we had it all ready for you to elope!' Mandy cried, in response to the bride's look of confusion.

'Anna…what…what are you doing…?'

Anna turned an angry glare on the nervously hovering Mr Sleighman. 'What do you think I am doing, you nasty little weed!'

He looked down at the ground and shuffled uncomfortably from foot to foot. 'I don't know…'

She stretched out a hand and gripped him by the chin, forcing him to lift his head. 'I'm eloping with a heavenly Russian artist, you dopy lapdog!'

Frowning, he pushed her hand away. 'Why…?'

'Because I love him!'

'But I love you…'

'You do not!'

'That Russian does not love you, I do…'

Anna slapped Mr Sleighman across the face. 'Shut your face, goat! The love Sasha bears for me is utterly pure and unselfish; anyone of sense can see that!'

'Calling names is not very nice…'

She slapped his other cheek. 'And neither are you, Mr Sleighman!'

'This isn't fair…I love you…'

'The feelings you have for me are nothing but lust and selfish desire!'

'But I'm a good Christian.'

She shoved him hard. 'What trash!'

He crumpled to the ground. 'That's not nice...' he whined, pulling his face up from the dirt.

She turned away in mute disgust.

The entire congregation had been watching this scene aghast. Anna heard a hushed, horrified whisper run through the wedding guests. She looked over her shoulder. Her father was advancing down the aisle towards her. His hands were clenched into fists and a black storm raged about his head.

'Mabel, where's my trousseau?' Anna shouted, lifting her dress's long skirts and starting to hurry onwards.

'Here, here!' a breathless voice replied from behind.

Anna was now going at a full gallop. She looked over her shoulder again. Mabel and Mandy were running along after her carrying the trunk between them, each with a hand through one of the side handles.

'I command you to stop, foolish child!' her father's bellow followed her.

Anna did not stop. She flew down the hill and onto the sandy wagon track leading down to the seashore. Her train and long, long white veil billowed out behind her like the tail of a comet speeding across the night sky. Just behind it came her two attendants, looking for all the world like two little angels following in the wake of their goddess as she flew across the heavens.

The bride and her breathless bridesmaids sped past the modest but smart two bay villa at the foot of the knoll, which was to have been her marital home. Mr Sleighman had spent the past few months anxiously furnishing it in readiness for housing his prized trophy, but it only took her a twinkling of an eye to pass the waiting house like a spirit fleeing the daybreak. As she passed, she kicked off the pinching, pointy-toed high-heeled shoes her feet were forced into.

Down, down to the seashore she ran, halting only when the lapping waters lay right at her bare toes. The sea had never seemed so wide or deep as it did now, when it stood between her and the man she loved. She could not see Ivanovsky, but the entire ship's crew had stopped work to stare at the strange spectacle of the runaway bride.

'What am I to do? What am I to do?' Anna wailed, wringing her hands in despair.

Mandy jumped up and down with glee and pointed to a bush just above the sands. 'A little boat, we have a little boat!'

'Yeah, get it!' cried Mabel.

The startled little wooden dinghy, which had been quietly sleeping in the warmth only moments before, was roughly hauled down to the water's edge in the fastest launch it had ever known. The trousseau was tossed in with careless abandon before Cupid's angels pushed the dinghy out until it floated. Then Mabel rushed to hold the bride's train and veil clear of the water while she waded out into the playful, frothing waves and boarded her not-so-grand barge with a grace befitting Queen Cleopatra. Then the two little oarswomen jumped in and began paddling franticly.

'Come on Mandy, you need to paddle faster!' screeched Mabel.

'Shut your cake-hole, Mabel! I'm paddling so fast my arm's sure to fall off!'

The tide had just begun to turn, and the surf was already rather boisterous. Several times the little dinghy's angelic young crew erupted into shrieks of alarm as large waves threatened to swamp it. The last and largest of the waves the seafarers passed through on their way out came heart-stoppingly close to overturning the little craft, but somehow they managed to get away with only a light dump of water into the boat.

Now that the breakers had been negotiated, the lace-and-frill attired little sailors really put their backs into it, and the little wooden dinghy skimmed across the ocean waves at a pace it had only ever dreamed about. Mostly in nightmares.

A rowdy cheer arose from the *Fearless One*'s watching crew. Anna now stood erect in the prow of the rapidly advancing craft, her veil streaming out behind her as it rested on the east wind. Many faces crowded the ship's rail. But Anna's eyes searched only for one face. Where was he? Where was her true bridegroom?

'Looks like we left somethin' behind, Mr Midshipman!' called a rough but cheerful voice.

'Yeah, looks like the newly-born Venus is keen to swap 'er clamshell for a more seaworthy vessel!'

The watching sailors all roared with laughter. The little wooden dinghy had been rowed within forty paces of the *Fearless One* by its now puffing, dishevelled little crew, who slowed their paddling to a more dignified pace.

Still Anna's desperate eyes had not alighted on Ivanovsky's beloved face. Where was he? Surely he *was* aboard the ship?

Then a sailor called out, 'There ya are, Mr Ivanovsky! You've been missin' all the fun.'

Anna could have cried with relief when Sasha's silver-maned head finally came into view. It looked as though he had just come up from his cabin. His hat, coat and gloves were absent and his waistcoat unbuttoned.

She saw him gasp as his eyes alighted on her, and a moment later the heavenly smile she loved so much lit up his face. 'Anya, can it really be you?'

'So *this* is the lucky gentleman Venus is so intent on marryin'!' called out some smart-Alec.

Anna barely heard the roar of laughter that greeted this latest witticism. Her world at that moment contained nothing except Sasha's utterly loving, profoundly joyous face. As Mabel and Mandy expertly docked their heroic little craft alongside the *Fearless One*, Anna reached out for the rope ladder hanging down the ship's side.

But before she mounted this stairway to happiness, she held out over the waters the bouquet of white Madonna lilies she had been clutching all this time, and gently let them drop onto the dancing sea. The ocean received this thanksgiving offering with a happy hiss of frothy bubbles rising to the surface.

Then the bride stepped onto the ladder and nimbly climbed aboard the *Fearless One*.

Sasha stood waiting to receive Anna with tears in his tender brown eyes and his arms open to embrace her. With a little cry of joy, she flung her arms around his neck.

'Oh Anya, my Anya, how I love you...'

At that moment, a swirling breath from the leaping breeze tossed

Anna's long veil into the air and enwrapped the bride and her true love in its gauzy, snowy-white folds. Anna's eyes shone with joy as she lifted a delicate hand to her beloved's cheek. And gazed solemnly up at him, she ran wonder-filled, feather-light fingers across the beautiful plain. 'Sasha, I love you. You are my true bridegroom; I give myself to you for eternity...'

Alone with Anna in the white, light-filled world created by the veil's embrace, a tear overflowed the unfathomably deep brown eyes that overflowed with love. 'There are no words to say what my heart feels...' he murmured, cradling her head in his hands.

Anna's delicate fingers wiped away the tears running down the beloved cheeks with a touch as ethereal as a sunbeam drying the morning dew from a blossom. 'Sasha, will you marry me?'

A smile of melting tenderness alighted on his sensitive, perfectly formed lips. 'The answer, you know it already, dear one...'

Like a honeybee reaching for the flower's nectar-filled heart as the white petals chastely embrace it, Anna reached up to the lips of the lover whose arms held her close, and lingeringly tasted their divine sweetness.

13

Rhyming Song

ANNA looked unwaveringly into the face of the wind that buffeted her and tried to filch her close-tied hat. Tossing seas filled the entrance of Wellington Harbour's mouth, and spray leapt into the air where the waves found their path impeded by the dark rocks of Barrett's Reef rearing from the ocean out in the channel. Dark, seaweed-crusted rocks ringed the shore near where Anna sat, with a long finger of them reaching out into the sea at the little cape's end. The vigorous southerly wind delighted in driving the waves onto the shore like herds of leaping, snorting, snowy-white horses with wild manes of foaming spray streaming behind them.

Turning her collar up and burrowing her hands deeper into her fur muff, she quietly laughed off the wind as it nipped and tugged at her. A sun that burned low behind scudding clouds and wandering mist broke through in places, creating a beautiful rainbow arch to bridge the turbulent waters, and scattering sunbeams that kissed the raindrops floating down over the distant hills into golden glitter. The snow-capped mountain peaks of the South Island, which the dancing open waters of Cook Strait ended in on a clear day, were hidden in vaporous veil.

Anna turned her eyes to closer marvels. Sasha stood before a well-fortified easel, his brush doing its usual fairy-light dance of magic that brought into being wondrous visions of light and colour. The awe-filled delight of watching him paint was still with her. The colour-bearing brush glided, swept, floated and tripped over the surface. Sometimes the lightning-quick brush would pause while a finger lifted or blended with a speedy sureness she could scarcely imagine possessing. Already the beauteous scene before Anna was captured with a mastery and feeling she could only marvel at. She sighed happily and settled more comfortably on the picnic blanket and cushion she sat on, then returned to the volume of Keats' poetry she was reading.

'Anya, are you ever going to read that letter?'

Anna looked up to find Sasha seated on a smooth boulder beside her. 'It has been only a week since this letter arrived,' she replied, fretfully fingering the letter lodged between the pages of her book.

He laughed quietly. 'Only? Are you waiting for ink to fade and paper to crumble first, *mllaya moyna?*'

She pulled out the still-sealed letter and regarded it hostilely. 'Do not tease me, or I shall become cross.'

He sat down behind the cushion she reclined on and put his arms around her. 'You must stop worrying about what your relatives think. You have created family of your own—' He paused to place a kiss on her cheek. 'And your husband hates to see you sad.'

She leaned her head back against his shoulder and sighed. 'But Jennifer can be so mean. Even the hand she wrote this address in looks jerky with rage and disappointment.'

The squeeze his encircling arms gave her was a little admonishing. 'Darling, stop thinking and do instead.'

'But I don't want to do.'

'Do anyway.'

Anna cast a despairing look at the letter. 'But they all hate me now, I know they do! And Jen will be full of talk of—of *him*.' For some reason, she could not bear to say Mr Sleighman's name, or hear it spoken.

'Then *I* shall do deed,' said Sasha, and before she could stop him the letter was in his hand.

'No, I am not ready!' she wailed, reaching for the letter.

But he held the letter too high for her to reach, and the effortlessly firm arm around her waist prevented any height being gained. 'You will never be ready because you have no wish to be. If you will not allow me to read it, I shall throw it into sea. You cannot let it stretch your mind on rack forever.'

Anna struggled against him for a few brief moments, then suddenly yielded to his restraining arm as the fear in her heart yielded to her will. 'Very well, read out the denouncement,' she said bleakly. 'I can conveniently throw myself into the sea from here if the need should arise.'

This melodramatic addition was tactfully, if long-sufferingly, ignored, and quickly the letter was unsealed and unfolded. He began reading it out:

Dear sister,

Mother and I are appreciative of the fact that you designed to take the great trouble of informing us that you arrived safely in Wellington, and that Mr Ivanovsky has conceded to make an honest woman of you after you had been living in sin for only a brief period of time.

I must inform you that my disappointment is great. My faith in your dutifulness and rationality was clearly misplaced. I can only hope and pray that Mother's constitution is robust enough to withstand the terrible shock wrought by your selfish and shameless act. To have brought a child up with such love and care only to have her throw her life away to some lowly barbarian is a horror I can only imagine.

 I hope that God will forgive you for the hurt and shame you have brought on your poor fiancé. Mr Sleighman is beside himself with grief at his beloved's cruel betrayal. Jilting such a decent, kind-hearted man on what he hoped was the happiest day of his life is a sin which I cannot easily forgive.

 When the unchristian, error-filled wretch you have designed to waste yourself upon finally abandons you, know that the repentant sheep, even though destitute and sin-stained, will be welcomed back into the fold.

I remain your dutiful sister

Mrs John Brown

By the time Sasha finished reading out the letter, Anna was huddled with her hands over her eyes. His warm, full tones gave the biting words a softness they scarcely deserved, but without them, she would not have been able to hear it out.

She felt his arms around her shoulders. 'Anya, you knew this would be result. I did too. It is why I could not beg you to come. I could not look into your eyes and tell you all would be well if only you follow your heart.'

She lifted her head from where it was buried in the arms resting on her up-drawn knees and looked at Sasha, who knelt before her. Her lower lip quivered with painful emotion, and her glistening eyes were unblinking. 'I will never be able to go back, to return to my home...'

He clasped her cold, trembling hands in his warm, steady ones. 'No, Anya, you will never be able to return to your former home. I am sorry for this.'

She pressed her lips tightly together and smiled through her sadness as she squeezed his hands. 'Now I know that Russians are correct about life being filled with bittersweetness. The old must always die so that the new can arise, just as the leaves of autumn must ever fade so that the spring may come once more. What moment of birth is not a moment of death also?'

Her smile was mirrored in his own tenderly concerned face. 'You are not regretful for leaving family and only home you knew?'

With her lips still tightly pressed to contain their hurt, she shook her head. 'I am a nomad now. Home is wherever you are, Sasha.'

He put his arms around Anna and drew her close. 'Oh *dragaya*, my *dragaya*...' His words were barely more than a sad sigh, and he finished by pressing a kiss to her cheek.

There was a companionable silence before he spoke once more. 'You know I intended to stay here in Wellington only one month before travelling southwards. I very much was looking forward to visiting South Island. What do you think about journeying south soon?'

She chewed her lip uncertainly as she looked at him. His longing eyes were fixed on the distant snowy peaks of the beginning of the South Island's mountain chain, which had silently been revealed by the lifting mist. She did not want to go. She was afraid. The mountains and lakes of the south were wild, rugged places, so she had heard. Travelling would be gruelling. And shops, there would be hardly any.

'The single room we are currently lodging in can scarcely be called adequate,' she replied, 'but surely the remote wilds of the South Island will offer only worse accommodation?'

'A gentleman I was acquainted with in Auckland offered me use of cottage on banks of Arrow River, in Central Otago. It has been unoccupied for a little while, but he assured me it is comfortable enough home.'

Anna swallowed hard. The thought of moving into a derelict cottage in the wild open wastes of Central Otago had no appeal. Very much the reverse, in fact. The idea was horrifying. The gold mining towns of Otago were reliably reported to be lawless places were drunkenness and brawling was rife.

'We are settled here. Perhaps next year...'

He had not removed his wistful eyes from the snow-capped mountains sitting so tantalisingly close. 'It is almost autumn now. Central Otago is said to be very beautiful in the autumn...'

'And also very cold,' she added with a shiver.

'Cold? In this land it is never cold.'

'But Central Otago is reported to be even colder then Wellington. Wellington is freezing, and it is summer here!'

'You Auckland dwellers really are rare breed of hothouse plant...' he sighed, reluctantly turning away from the distant peaks shimmering across the sea.

* * * *

A misty turquoise blue floated, and in the centre of it a hazy patch of bright red. Anna stretched and yawned, then focused her sleep-drowsy eyes. The turquoise blue morphed into an expanse of sea with a cloudless sky dipping into it on the horizon, and the red clarified into the red shirt Sasha was wearing as he stood, palette and brush in hand, before an easel placed in front of the window.

This red vision jolted her just-awoken mind. She frowned rather irritably. 'Sasha, why do you insist on wearing that shirt? The loose style is more smock than it ought, and the colour is not proper for a gentleman. White is much more becoming, in my view.'

He stilled his paint-heavy brush and glanced up with a soft smile that bore no reflection of her frown. 'Good morning, my sweet one. In Russia this is perfectly respectable attire.'

'For peasants, maybe. But you ought to dress like a proper gentleman.'

She caught the flicker of a bemused smile as he returned to his canvas. 'My mother and father *are* peasants.'

It was now ten O'clock, and she was far more awake than she would have liked at this hour of the morning. 'What?'

'They are better off peasants who own their own land, but they are people of the land, nevertheless.'

Having for some reason assumed that his background had been one of genteel poverty, perhaps a good family fallen on hard times, she sat up in bed with something of a jerk. 'Heavens, what would people think of me if I told them!'

His peace and good humour remained unruffled. 'More than if you told them your husband's maternal grandmother was a gypsy, I should imagine.'

'*What?*'

'Yes, she was wonderful woman. I remember how, as little boy, I used to sit on her knee as she sat beside the stove on long winter evenings and told me beautiful Russian folktales. My favourites were *Fair Vassilisa and Baba Yagá*, and *Ivan the Peasant's son and the Three Dragons.*' His eyes filled with the misty, faraway light of fond memories, and he stopped working and gazed out the window into the blue yonder. 'I got my dark eyes from her, you know.'

But Anna was too aghast at the thought of her own high-class blood mixing with that of peasants and gypsies to listen closely. 'Indeed!'

'Another favourite tale she used to tell was *Grandfather Frost*. I think you would enjoy it too, *lapooshka*. Would you like to hear?'

She drew her knees up and hugged them a little resentfully. 'Do I look like a child? Fairytales are for children.'

He put his palette down on the little table below the rimu-wood windowsill, picked up a cloth and thoughtfully began wiping the paint off his fingers. 'Yes.'

'Yes what?'

Smiling broadly, he tossed the cloth aside and threw himself down beside her on the bed. 'Yes, you do look like child when you frown like that.'

Her frown melted into resigned indifference, and she leaned back against the pillows. 'Fine, just tell it to me.'

'Well, once upon a time—'

'Do not be insulting.'

'But all good tales start in this way! Surely you are not too old for good tale?'

Her lip twitched as she unwillingly started cracking up. 'Fine, tell it to me like I am five years old. What do I care!'

His face danced with suppressed laughter. 'Thank you, my sweet one. So, once upon a time, there lived an old man and his second wife, and they each had a daughter. Although the wife indulged her own child, she treated her stepdaughter harshly. The old man's daughter was forced to rise before daybreak and do every domestic chore, yet the stepmother found fault with all she did and scolded whole day through. Even wildest wind grows calm with time, but not the old woman.

"Get rid of her, old man," she said to her husband one day. "I cannot bear sight of her any longer. Drive into forest with her and leave her in the snow."

'The old man pleaded, but as always, wife had her way. One bitterly cold morning he harnessed horses to sledge and called his daughter.

'When he reached lofty fir-tree deep in snowy forest, he stopped and, with heavy heart, left the poor girl trembling beside large snowdrift.

'The girl sat shivering beneath the hoary fir-tree. Then all of a sudden, she heard a cracking and snapping of twigs and she knew Grandfather Frost was leaping through the trees. In a twinkling, he leapt into topmost branches of very tree that she sat under.

"Are you warm, my pretty one?" he called.

"Yes, quite warm, thank you, Grandfather Frost," replied she.

'He swung down lower and cracking and snapping grew louder. "Are you warm?" he called again. "Are you snug, my pretty one?"

'Girl could barely breathe, but she said, "Yes, I'm quite warm, thank you, Grandfather Frost."

'Then he climbed lower still, and snapping and cracking of frosty boughs became very loud indeed. "Are you warm?" he asked. "Are you snug, my pretty one? Are you cosy, my sweet snow child?"

'The poor girl had grown so numb that she could barely move her tongue, but still managed to whisper, "I'm quite warm, thank you, Grandfather Frost."

'At this, Grandfather Frost was moved to pity by the poor girl, so he wrapped her in his thick furs.

'When old man went into snowy forest to bring his daughter's body home to be buried, he was astonished to find her sitting alive and well under lofty fir-tree. She was wrapped in costly furs over a velvet gown, and beside her set large chest overflowing with furs and rare gems. The overjoyed old man gathered his daughter and her treasures up and bore them home.

'When old woman saw the riches girl had won in forest, she was filled with amazement and envy. "Harness the horses, old man," says she. "Take my own daughter into forest and leave her in very same place."

'So old man did.

'Wife's daughter soon began to shiver and shake as cold seeped into her very marrow.

'Presently, Grandfather Frost came leaping through icy treetops. "Are you warm, my pretty one?" he called.

"No, I'm terribly cold!" replied she. "Be off with your pinching and piercing!"

'Snapping and crackling of branches became ever louder as Grandfather Frost descended. "Are you warm?" called he. "Are you snug, my pretty one?"

"I'm freezing!" she snapped. "Go away, you stupid old man!"

'But Grandfather Frost came down lower still and boughs cracked and snapped louder than ever as his breath grew colder and colder. "Are you warm?" he called again. "Are you snug, my pretty one? Are you cosy, my sweet one?"

"No!' cried she. "I'm frozen stiff! Be off with you, stupid greybeard!"

'At this, Grandfather Frost grew so angry that he breathed piercing cold blast over her, and she instantly was frozen into an iceblock. The end.'

Anna greeted 'the end' with a thoughtful silence.

But presently she looked up at her husband with brows knitted and eyes solemn. 'Sasha, I'm sorry I have been such a moaner for the past two months. This one room apartment is small and a great deal less grand than what I am used to, but it is a decent enough home. I'm sure no newly-wed husband can hear such complaints from his bride without a sting of hurt.'

He gave a quietly satisfied nod, then looked up at her with lines of laughter playing at the corners of his drowsy-lidded brown eyes. 'So, are you cosy, my sweet snow child?'

'Oh, too cruel!' she laughed, covering her shame-filled eyes with a hand.

'Are you snug, my pretty one?'

'Oh Sasha, I have to admit that I would have treated Grandfather Frost as the second girl did. But now I have been warned by her dreadful fate. So the answer is: I am quite warm, thank you, Grandfather Frost.'

Laughing, he embraced her tightly. 'I am afraid I am little low on costly furs and gems at moment, so you will have to make do with this instead—' He kissed her.

A little later on, Sasha disappeared downstairs to retrieve the breakfast their landlady provided for the tenants in her apartment building, which lacked individual cooking facilities.

Anna got up and began to dress. However, she only got as far as under-shift, stockings and drawers before she remembered that she no longer had a lady's maid to aid with the lacing of corsets and dresses. With her un-tightened corset loosely on, she sat down on the foot of the bed with a huff of annoyance and waited for her new lady's maid to return.

Presently he did. Scrambled eggs, tea and toast spread with marmalade steamed on the tray he carried.

She waited until he had put the tray down on the bed, which was the only surface not occupied by paint tubes, brushes, books, sheets of paper and canvases at various stages of compilation.

'Sasha, lace me up please,' she said, rising and turning her back towards him.

Holding a piece of partly eaten toast between his teeth, he drew the slackness out of the lacing.

Anna took hold of the bed frame. 'Pull harder.'

With another bite removed, he held the toast in one hand again. 'But this is already tight.'

'Do it harder.'

The toast was back between teeth and the laces were drawn gently snug.

'Harder, Sasha, harder.'

But this time, the laces did not move. 'This is tight enough.'

'No, put some strength into it—and get that toast out of your mouth! If a maid was so insolently casual she would have felt the back of my hand by now.'

He stood in front of her with his head tilted to one side and a dark eyebrow raised. 'Go on then, hit me.'

Her mouth opened to launch the heated retort poised on the tip of her tongue, but then fell silently shut. Snapping at someone enshrouded in such an aura of casualness and unshakable serenity could only result in one thing. One would look a hot-tempered fool, the sort of person who kicks a mountain because it is hard to climb. She settled for a challenging glare at her husband instead, with a supporting cast of hands on hips.

The drowsy-lidded eyes only spoke of eternal patience and mild bemusement. It was infuriating.

She turned away with a huff that signalled defeat. 'I see. You do know that most of my dresses will not fit with a half-on corset?'

'Let them out. I refuse to torture my own wife.'

She flung the trunk open with an unnecessary amount of force, and revelled in the loud bang this caused. A set of petticoats were bitterly snatched and violently tugged on, and then a bright blue gown was seized. She stepped into it, fiercely hauled it up onto her arms, then presented its unlaced front to Sasha in pointed silence.

He carefully put down the second piece of toast, and then painstakingly wiped his fingers on a napkin. After this, he smoothed his hair down, and lastly cleared his throat. 'Does your slave pass inspection, princess?'

No, he was not going to get the better of her. He was not going to do it. She quickly looked down. But it was too late. His mock-grovelling manner had done its damage, and her fine palace of self-conscious hurt and feminine indignity crumbled into a ruined rubble of helpless laughter.

He quietly laughed with her as he gently drew her laces snug. 'There, that is perfect.'

After Anna had piled her brunette locks up in a high, loose bun and arranged her fringe and the few loose tendrils around her ears, both of which she curled into tight ringlets with a heated poker, she set down beside the breakfast tray.

While she poured a cup of tea, Sasha walked over to the scotch chest by the door and picked up the letters he had left on it when he entered.

She winced at the sound his booted feet made on the thin, blue, almost threadbare Persian rug covering the centre of the room's wooden floorboards. 'Sasha, the din those riding boots make is tiresome. Riding boots are not appropriate footwear for indoors. Why do you insist on wearing them constantly?'

Letters in hand, he paused, and she thought she caught the sound of a slightly weary sigh. 'These boots I bought when I lived among Cossacks for a year, and they have become like old friend. Unbroken is their faithfulness in keeping dusty and muddy streets at bay and carrying me over plains and up mountains in pursuit of my muse.'

Nothing except the break-neck speed of the revolutions of her stirring teaspoon gave a clue to her state of mind. 'Was this before or after the time you spent studying in Vienna?'

'Before.' He now stood in front of her, holding out two letters. 'These came in this morning's post. To you they are addressed.'

She took them with the hesitance of someone taking hold of a pot-handle that they are unsure about the temperature of. 'And the other letter is for you?' she asked, glancing at the very thick letter he retained.

'Yes,' he replied with a pleased smile. 'It is from my mother.'

While he sat engrossed in his mother's letter in the room's only armchair, which he had just relieved of its pile of canvases, Anna toyed fitfully with her own mail.

With a hint of envy, she watched varying degrees of joy, sadness, homesickness and loving gratification pass over her husband's face as he read his mother's words. How wonderful it must be to receive such tender outpourings of a mother's love; to receive love rather than the hate and disappointment that was her own family's sole gift.

With a bitter frown, she turned her attention to her own letters. The first one was addressed in a large, slightly uneven hand. This was not the hand of any Browns, so she opened it with relative composure. The letter was written on a purple letter paper with a wide border of vines, roses and chubby winged cherubs.

Dear Anna,

Us two were delirious with joy when we heard from your sister that you are now Mrs Sasha Ivanovsky. Well done, well done, well done!!!!!

The big drama you made of slapping that cheater across the face at the church door was topping fun. We are in awe. The way all the grown-ups flapped about wringing their hands and weeping and raging and moaning was such a bore. You made a super runaway bride. How could anyone not think so?! What you did was so romantic and wild and bold!!! Eloping is a thrilling thing. Elopers are super!

Everyone was very cross with us for having helped you escape. Mother sentenced us to a fortnight of no pudding. But even if Mother's resolve had lasted more than the one day it did before pudding was back, it would still have been worth it!

We miss you and Sasha loads and beg- please, please, please!- that you will both write soon and tell us how you are getting on. We are sure you have had piles of super adventures, and we are dying to hear!

You are AMAZING, and us two send absolute mountains of good wishes and love and hugs!

Very BEST wishes for everything

Mabel and Mandy

P.S — *this is just for Sasha:* thank you ever so much for the drawing of us two. It is such a good likeness! But we had a hard time hunting it down with the clues you gave, clever-clogs!

This sincere, delightfully exuberant letter made Anna smile. She really had been too hard on them. Mabel and Mandy were such an adorable pair, even if they were brats of the first order.

When she moved onto the second letter, the warm fuzziness left by the reading of the first rapidly fled. Although she could not place the hand that had addressed it, the nervous, spidery crawl that scrawled out the address breathed a musty, deathly cold into her heart, which jumped in dread. Something about the scent clinging grimly to the paper bred revulsion. It seemed unpleasantly familiar, like a horrid dream lurking just beyond recollection. Forcing her quaking fingers still, she tore the letter open and unfolded it. Imprisoning the breath filling her lungs, she began to read.

Dear Anna,

It is good that you have finally told us where you are. We were worried. A naive young woman is vulnerable without her reletives to protect her honour. I do not understand your leaving our wedding like that. The things you said to me were hurtful. I know you did not mean them. A chaste and pure lady like you is bound to be shy about marriage. The female brain is subject to irational thoughts and strange urges. When this fevered state gets hold of a nervous female it is dangerous and unpredictable. I prayed to God. He told me you were bestowed on me as my wife by Him. You disobeyed the will of Our Lord by running away. You will be punished for it. The man you are with is a lowly beast who is going to treat you badly. He will drink the demon drink and beat you until you beg for mercy. He will shout abuse at you until you cry. He will throw hot water at you. He will force his vile body on your trembling frightened modesty ▬. God created you to be my wife. He said you belong to me. The marriage you say you had ▬ with this man is a lie. He will have lied to you. You are married not in the eyes of God or the law. ▬ Stop living in sin. Repent. God is merciful. Praise His name, for He is merciful. Helleluya. Praise His holy name. I'm coming for you. I'm coming to save you. Save you in Jesus' name. Amen. I love you. I love you more then he does ▬ Then the foul beast does. I think about you all day and night. Think about him having you. Having your ▬ I'm coming.

I'm coming for you. I'm coming for the thing God has given me. I'm His loyal son. I praise His name. I pray to Him. His angels fly around in my head. they are everywhere in me.

Hellaluya.

I'm coming.

your intended, Norris Derek Sleighman

'I must get some air!' gasped Anna, dashing for the door with the letter clutched in her rigid hand.

She barely made it to the back garden before she was violently sick.

It was so vile, so unspeakably horrid. The man was as mad as a rabid dog. His words, the mere thought of him, made her skin crawl and her breath catch in her throat. She believed she had separated herself from him for eternity. But now he was climbing out of his worm-filled coffin like some undead soul and snuffling out the scent of her warm blood. The leech had been cheated out of the meal he thought was his, and now he was clearly intent on hunting down the escaped feast. The horrors that the letter bred in her mind were so vile and lurid that Anna could not bear to look at them. She could not speak his name even in her own mind.

Crushing the letter into a tight ball with ice-cold hands, she pushed it deep into her pocket, and the thoughts of *him* deep into her subconscious. Any time one of them reared above the surface it was brutally thrust back down into the murky depths.

The day passed without Anna having spoken of the letter to either Sasha or herself. She was determined to treat the letter much like one would treat a rotting carcass lying in the path one was travelling. By holding one's breath, averting one's eyes and hurrying past.

But the trouble was that this rotting carcass followed her around like a shadow. Every time she turned, there it was right behind her.

When darkness fell, she was too afraid to go to sleep. His loathsome urges might reach out across the borderless, timeless dreamscape and sink their engorged, blood-seeking lips into her.

Sleep was a friend that often was reluctant to visit Anna. So on this night, as on others when sleep shunned her, she sat in bed with her knees drawn up to her chin and silently watched her husband sleeping.

Outside, the wind had fallen still. The round moon hung low over the rippling sea, casting a silver stairway that led all the way up to the sad, serene countenance that smiled quietly down on the velvet night. Wispy scraps of cloud scudded across the moon's face like dreams across a slumberer's mind. The moonbeams cast earthwards by their serene celestial mother stole breathlessly in through the window and alighted on Sasha's silver mane, and together the two united into glittering threads of pale, pure silver of such magic they belonged not to the earthly, but to the celestial heavens. The moonbeams that alighted on the peaceful slumberer's softly, secretively smiling face cast a spell that turned him into an angel. For that was what she saw when she gazed down at him. A heavenly angel sleeping in her bed.

Anna's own soul was a stranger to the peace her slumbering angel rested on. Like bats that unfurl their leathery wings and take flight in the shadowy dusk, thoughts of *him* circled about her cringing head in the darkness. Every time one of their dreadful wings brushed against her consciousness, a tremor of revulsion coursed through her heart.

When the midnight hour struck, she reached a resolve. Turning towards the divine sleeper, she placed a thin, shaky hand on the smooth silver skin of his chest.

'Sasha, wake up,' she whispered, rocking him gently.

The celestial slumberer slept on, merely lifting his lips into an angelic smile like an angel into whose ear God had whispered a divine secret.

She shook him a little harder. 'Sasha, wake up.'

This time his head stirred slightly, but his eyelids did not lift.

She leaned down over him and kissed his smiling lips. She felt them stir beneath her, and after another kiss from her, they gently responded. A drowsy arm embraced her as he slowly kissed her back.

Then the eyelids lifted, and dark brown eyes regarded her with a drowsiness that contained utter alertness in its depths. 'Yes, my love?'

With her hand cupping his cheek and face hovering just above his, she solemnly looked down into his eyes. 'Sasha, let us travel south.'

He smiled a smile that would have been puzzled if it had not been so pleased. 'This is what you wish?'

'Yes.'

'How soon do you desire to leave, my little rabbit?'

'How soon can you be ready?'

His dark brows lifted slightly in surprise. 'Well…late tomorrow it would be possible for me to be ready.'

'This sounds good. Go down to the wharf and book us a passage to the South Island first thing tomorrow.'

His warm, steady fingers traced gentle lines over her cheeks. 'What is this sudden hurry? Is all well with you, my love?'

She slowly ran her hands through his thick, silky mane, and smiled down on him. 'Sasha, I do love you. And I am sorry I scold you and moan constantly.'

'Do not trouble yourself about this, little darling. Following this path, it is not easy for you.'

'Know that I have never, not for even one moment, regretted marrying you. I have not felt as happy as you have made me since I was a carefree little girl.'

His smiled turned a little teasing. 'I cannot with ease imagine my solemn-eyed Anya as ever having been carefree little girl.'

She allowed herself a quiet chuckle, but quickly returned to seriousness. 'Sasha, the way you calmly flout the rules of society when you wish, and quietly go about living life your way makes me afraid sometimes. That is why I nag you to conform.'

'I know. It is a primal fear. Sheep that is apart from flock is the one wolf sets his eyes on. But the good shepherd always watches over his flock. The fearful must have faith and trust in that.'

Anna nodded. And at that moment she resolved to embrace her

new life as well as her new husband. No longer was she Miss Anna Brown, the daughter of one of the colony's foremost families. Now she was Mrs Anya Ivanovsky, wife of a humbly placed but gifted artist. The wife of a beautiful, kind and intelligent man who loved her.

14

Kalinka

THE steamship passage from Wellington to Dunedin was delightful in its uneventfulness. The city of Dunedin, situated about three-quarters of the way down the South Island's East Coast, was the largest of the South Island towns, eclipsing Auckland for the title of New Zealand's premier city.

Here, Anna and Sasha, and the four trunks that contained all their worldly possessions, boarded a stagecoach travelling towards the Otago goldfields. The stagecoach being filled to capacity, Sasha and the two other younger men had to take the rooftop. As for Anna, she was squeezed between a freshly emigrated seamstress with a baby in her arms, and an elderly gentleman of generous girth with sideburns to match. Two white-haired, black-suited gentlemen of distinguished and austere appearance, who proved to be lawyers, occupied the seat opposite.

Anna thought it most ungallant of the two perched like a pair of crows on their spacious seat that they did not allow the gentleman beside her to join them. Lounging there while two ladies (or in Anna's view, a lady and a woman) sat right before them jammed up like hens in an overcrowded henhouse was an unspeakable act, and Anna responded by only ever looking at the perpetrators from down the end of a sniffily up-turned nose, and refraining from conversing with them.

A pale coating of dust soon covered Anna's clothes, and an erosion of her nerves by the seamstress' baby's constant wailing more than doubled her grief at this unprivileged mode of travel. But mindful of the fate of the old woman's cross, sharp-tongued daughter at Grandfather Frost's hands, Anna tried her very best to keep her sunny side up. Only the merest grimace escaped her when the lurching of the stagecoach drove two elbows, one small and sharp, the other big and brawny, into her sides.

The road passed along the rolling coastal hills for some miles before turning west and heading into the interior.

At the little town of Lawrence, the unmannered crows were shed. After a night spent at the stage post, which provided only the barest essentials—or not, depending on one's view—a new passenger boarded. He at first seated himself on the bench previously occupied by the barbarian loungers, but upon catching a whiff of alcohol on the unshaven, roughly-dressed traveller's breath, the keen-eyed little seamstress ordered him up on the roof in no uncertain terms.

Anna was most impressed. She herself would have spent the entire journey with an expression of glacial disapproval frozen onto her face instead.

The expulsion of this more mature man resulted in the coachman offering Sasha and the seamstress' husband a seat inside. But while Sasha gladly moved inside, the other man did not. He and his wife appeared to be experiencing some degree of marital strife, and he sharply declined the offer. Clinging to the high, lurching roof of a speeding stagecoach along with a pile of luggage and a drunk with a bent stovepipe hat seemed much preferred by him to the company of his darling wife.

The lush green farmland of Otago's periphery had now been swapped for a drier, stonier landscape of browns and yellows dotted with a tree's occasional green. At Raes Junction, the road inland joined the Clutha River and followed it all the way up to the town of Alexandra. This town was in a tussock-covered basin ringed by tall mountain ranges.

Anna had never seen its like. The wild, wide-open spaces seemed to stretch on forever. Even the skies here felt bigger, higher, bluer. In this place Nature ruled supreme, and humans seemed but a speck on a primal world. Anna was really not sure she enjoyed feeling like a speck. God had created man last, and upon him placed the purpose of being master of all that had come into being on the first five days of creation. This vast, timeless landscape was not right. There was not much mastering going on here.

Anna drew in close beside her husband, and wished, not for the first time, that he would desist from practically hanging out the window as he gaped in awe at the passing vistas.

'Sasha, are we almost there yet?'

With his face still alight with wonder, he pulled his attention off the landscape for the first time that morning. 'All going well, two more days should find us at Arrowtown,' he replied, putting his arm around her.

She snuggled into his comforting strength and breathed in the manly but opulent fragrance clinging to his coat. 'Sasha, it is so empty here. Is Arrowtown like this too?'

'I believe it to be somewhat similar, although it is in a more mountainous place.'

'I don't like it here. There are no houses, no shops, no people, no civilisation.'

'But it is beautiful! Do you not think so, *doosha maya*?'

'Yes, Sasha,' she said unconvincingly. 'But I much prefer Auckland.'

He laughed a quiet, bemused laugh. 'But of course! All people of your little—*pardon moi, great* city— believe it to be most perfect of places.'

Anna was aware that she was almost certainly pouting, but she did not care. 'This place is unnerving.'

'To be before nature is to be before spiritual. It is right to tremble in such holy presence, but to turn from nature is to turn from the Divine, to turn from our primal mother, from whence we all come.'

'But there is *nothing* here,' was Anna's slightly whining reply.

'In Russia, we think of the place that gives us our existence as mother. We talk of this place as Mother Steppe, Mother Neva River, and so on. Many cultures that have not yet severed their primal bond with nature think of land in this way. The native people of New Zealand talk of earth as being primal mother that gave birth to humankind in the very beginning.'

Anna gave a contemptuous huff. 'Such bonds with the land are well and good for primitive tribes, but more civilised peoples have moved past that. We seek to tame nature and bend her to our will.'

A rhythmic snoring arose from the far corner of the opposite seat, where the portly, side-burned gentleman's nodding head had sunk to his chest.

'It is not right to think thus,' Sasha replied quietly. 'The relationship between land and people should be one of love and cooperation, not domination and submission. Much like good relationship between husband and wife.'

'But it is a wife's lot to be subordinate to her husband. Just as Jesus Christ is head of the church, a husband is rightfully head of the home. A happy home is one where the man is undisputed lord and master. Like a strong yet benevolent king, the head of the household ensures a domain where everyone knows their role and disputes are quickly settled.'

Sasha laughed quietly. 'This theory of yours, it is a phantom that never materialises in your actions.'

Anna lifted her head from his shoulder and rested an indignant eye on him. 'Are you calling me a bad wife?'

The lines around his eyes danced with laughter, and a moment later his lips lit up in a broad smile that tried not to be. 'No, *doosha maya*, not bad wife, just insubordinate one.'

Frowning, she rested her head back on his shoulder then gave him a cross thump on the chest with a closed hand. Nevertheless, she said no more. He was quite right, of course. She was anything but a meek little wife who bent to her husband's will like a birch sapling in the wind. For one thing, it is very difficult to bend in the wind if it refuses to blow. And for another, she hated being ordered around and only did things she did not wish to under extreme duress and always with a bad grace. As the stagecoach rattled on, she pondered on her failings as a good Christian wife in silence.

* * * *

After a stop at the mining settlement of Clyde, the road continued west, passing between the Garvie Mountains and the Dunstan Mountains. The road's progress followed the course of the big, wild Clutha River's stony bed up to the slightly larger mining settlement of Cromwell, where it left the Clutha River behind and swapped to following the smaller Kawarau River. At the junction of the Kawarau and Arrow Rivers, the stagecoach turned off the road that led to Queenstown and followed this smaller river.

Empty hills clothed in tussock and wild thyme wandered as far as the eye could see. The strange forms carved out of the schist rock by the wild winds that often raced over the land gave these hills and mountains an even more eerie appearance. The schist tors were everywhere in the stony landscape, rearing up in the most unexpected places in forms that the imagination could turn into beasts, spears, tables and spectres with ease. Even though it was only the beginning of March, the tall mountains looming on almost every horizon were capped with snow that shimmered against clear blue skies.

Anna was exhausted by the sleepless nights spent in bare hotel rooms that were surprisingly cold at night considering the heights the mercury soared to during the day. The endless jolting and rattling as the coach passed over the dusty, rutted road had finished the sleep-deprived traveller off.

By the final day, she started to regularly nod off to sleep from ten in the morning. But every time she drifted off to sleep, the jolt of the stagecoach passing over a dry rut had her wide awake before the sleep could give her any refreshment. If anything, she awoke even more tired than she fell asleep.

By late that hot, cloudless afternoon, she felt as parched, dusty and flat as the road itself. Even the stagecoach's rattling and jolting could not fend sleep off any longer. Stupefied by the dusty, sweltering heat, she fell into a fitful sleep.

But not for long. This time a warm, gentle voice called her back. 'Anya darling, wake up.'

Anna let out a weak moan of protest at the hand gently shaking her. 'Go away...'

'Anya, we are at our journey's end.'

Anna lifted her head with a jolt. Now very much awake, she realised that the stagecoach had stopped. In a sudden panic to see the dreaded place that was to be her home, she started up and made for the coach's open door. The coachman stood at the bottom of the lowered step holding out a hand to assist her down. Only lightly touching the offered hand, she sprung nimbly down.

The place the stagecoach had stopped at was a flat dotted with willows, larches, sycamores and silver birches and surrounded by mountains, some close, some distant. Along the roadside stood a fence built of long shards of schist rock set in the earth and threaded with wires that ran through holes bored in the rock. A little wooden gate led up an overgrown path that disappeared into trees speckled with the first golden autumn leaves.

Filled with nervous anticipation, she could hardly wait while the coachman unloaded the luggage. What ruined horror was to be her home? What deprivations awaited?

However, by the time the stagecoach was rattling into the distance with a cloud of dust in attendance, her thoughts had progressed. Even the meanest, most primitive hovel was preferable to a grand palace entered as Mrs Sleigh—*him*.

Anna lifted her chin and straightened her expression. Yes, whatever else this new home might prove to be, it was a long, long way from that whimpering dog, that slimy reptile.

No one in New Zealand knew where Mr and Mrs Ivanovsky were really going. Of that Anna had made sure. It would doubtless take *him* a very long time, and a great many miles, to figure out that she was not in Kaitaia. This false lead had been an inspired idea that suddenly came to her just as she was dashing for the steamboat. Initially, she had intended to vanish without a word to anyone. But now, instead of going to Wellington, he would hurry to Kaitaia instead. Being the North Island's northern-most town, this would take him as far away from her as it was possible to get without leaving the country. It was perfect.

Anna rubbed her hands together in glee. When enough time to

reach Kaitaia and bumble around there fruitlessly for a good while had passed, he would get a letter from his former intended informing him that she was living in Alice Springs, the Australian Outback, where Sasha had abandoned her and fled to Sydney with a convict girl.

Seizing the two lighter trunks, Anna almost laughed aloud in fiendish delight at these happy and gratifying thoughts. Mabel and Mandy would have been proud.

She followed Sasha, who carried the other two trunks, through the gate. Once she had negotiated the strand of trees beside the front fence, Anna found herself standing in a grassy clearing. A small cottage built of schist stone and mud brick rose before her. The front of the cottage almost looked like a face, she fancied. The two windows on either side were the eyes, the yellow-painted wooden door in the centre the nose, and the gabled corrugated tin roof the cap. Although humble and a little forlorn in its overgrown clearing, the tiny cottage seemed a happy, welcoming house.

'Your new home, it pleases you?'

Anna turned to her quietly relieved-looking husband. 'Yes, Sasha, it pleases me.'

'I am glad, Anya.'

Anna smiled to herself and looked down. 'And I am sure our children will like it too.'

Uncertain joy flickered across Sasha's face. 'You...you are with child?'

Her smile broadened as she looked up at him. 'Yes, Sasha, you are going to be a father early next spring.'

His face lit up. 'Oh Anya, that is wonderful!'

'I know you will be a marvellous father to our baby.'

The Ivanovskys soon stood on the flat stone slab that was the doorstep, she impatiently waiting while he searched his pocket for the keys. When he had finally found the key and turned it in the lock, she opened the door and made to step into the dusky hall.

But a gently restraining hand took hold of her arm. 'No, my *kalinka*, wait.'

'What does *kalinka* mean?' she asked, turning to find Sasha smiling down on her.

'Kalinka is the guilder rose, Russian symbol of young bride. This is your first home as a bride. You must permit me to carry you over the threshold.'

A cloud of nervous reluctance blotted out her smile, but the sun shone again after only a moment. Of course Sasha would not drop her or accidentally bludgeon her to death against the wall. He was a true man, not a crazed, obnoxious fool like—like that *thing*.

Filled with the sudden realisation that she trusted Sasha utterly, Anna dropped the two trunks she held and put her arm around his shoulder. 'Of course you must. One cannot go against tradition in these matters. If one does, the butter will never set or some such dreadful thing.'

'Oh Anya, I love it when you joke!' he laughed, lifting her into his arms with ease.

'I was not—' began Anna, who had remained poker-faced throughout the utterance, but then she started to laugh. 'And I love it when you are strong and manly!'

He gave her a toss that made her shriek and cling more tightly to his shoulders, then stepped over the threshold. 'Welcome home, *mllaya moyna.*'

Epilogue

PICKING up the two tin pails resting near the backdoor, Anna made her way across the carpet of bright-hued autumn leaves covering the clearing. She passed the washhouse and other assorted simple stone outbuildings, then continued down the sloping path.

After skirting the flaming larch and sycamore trees that held out their over-friendly arms, she passed under a stately weeping willow that dipped its reverently bowing boughs into the chattering Arrow River. Upon reaching the pebbly riverbed, she stepped onto a flat boulder at the crystal-clear, swiftly flowing river's edge and knelt to fill her pails with the always-icy water. So that the pails would not overburden her thin arms, she filled them only to halfway.

This task done, the little water-carrier set the pails at her feet and rested her eyes on the river. It was a friendly river, she had decided. Pleasantly active without being hurried, absent of murkiness, prettily pebbled and fringed by delightful trees that bejewelled the gliding waters with the leaves sacrificing their lives in a final flaming blaze of glory. The Arrow River was reassuringly shallow too. Not much risk of suffering the 'New Zealand death', or 'Otago disease' as it was known here, unlike in the much larger, swifter Clutha River.

Nevertheless, it was cold, she added to herself with a shiver. This she knew from unwilling firsthand experience. One especially hot afternoon not long after they had moved in, Sasha had suggested she join him in a cooling dip. She, of course, expressed horror at this idea. What of the eels? The sharp stones? The biting fish? But Sasha, having spent days listening to her moan about how hot she was, had seized hold of Anna and thrown her in. She felt sure that her shriek had been heard in Queenstown.

Unable to smother a smile at the memory despite herself, Anna lifted her pails and turned for home.

That had been one year ago. Now, the little cottage was home to four Ivanoskys. Though not for a few hours today. Tatiana and Natasha were currently in the care of Mrs Dodson, the goldminer's wife who lived in the cottage a little further down the Arrow River.

Once she had set the pails down on the kitchen floor, Anna wiped her hands dry on her apron. Looking around the small kitchen, a sense of quiet satisfaction settled on her. Now that the spiders had been evicted and their many webs demolished, the dust thrown out and the wooden floorboards scrubbed, the little cottage looked quite a cheerful, homely dwelling. The furniture left by the previous occupants—a stout, well-worn kitchen table, an iron-framed double bed, a battered trunk living at the foot of the bed, a scotch chest with several handles missing, a cracked dressing mirror, and a few simple chairs—provided the bare essentials of living.

At least the curtains were there to add a touch of comfort, she thought with a sigh. The yellow gingham ones hanging in the kitchen gave it a pleasantly cheerful air, and the white, blue daisy-patterned curtains adorning the parlour and two little bedrooms were delightfully fresh.

Now that she had finished admiring the results of her earlier labours, Anna turned to the task she had placed before herself. She had resolved to be a proper housewife today and spend the day cooking. When she was not cleaning the house and washing the clothes, or watching over the sleeping twins, she spent most of her days accompanying Sasha on his painting expeditions. Often he painted the river, either here at the bottom of the garden, or travelled further along its banks to capture different views and moods. And when he did not do this, he walked up into the hills to paint.

Delightful as it was to spend the day thus, it was not proper for a wife to have her husband do all the cooking. Not proper at all. The fact that she could not cook Anna saw as no impediment. She had armed herself with *Mrs Beeton's Book of Household Management*. Besides, if all these common girls could manage it, why could not she?

In addition to duty, there was another thing spurring her to the stove. She was fed up with eating Russian peasant fare. *Kasha*, which translates as 'mash', was the worst. It was any grain—millet (or birdseed, as she called it), buckwheat, semolina or oats—boiled into a mash and flavoured with any combination of sweet or savoury additions. *Kasha* was fit only for horses.

It had got to the point where she had dreams about beef Wellington, salmon mousse and Victoria sponge, and nightmares about kasha, cabbage soup and potato pancakes.

She had decided to begin her culinary expedition with a white loaf and the making of blackberry jam. Sasha made only traditional black bread, which was so dark and heavy that it surely was almost indigestible. Had not the good Dr Bramell himself told her that people of frail stature and delicate nerves such as her should eat only the finest white bread? Anything else would overtax a delicate constitution, he pronounced. As for the blackberry jam, the large supply of ripe fruit provided by the bushes growing rampantly along the riverbank made the making of blackberry jam the only decent thing to do.

Two boys belonging to the miner and his wife living a little further downstream had been paid with a few coins and a large bowl of leftover kasha to fill a large pail with blackberries. This brimming pail now set waiting on the kitchen table. But before the cooking could commence, The Stove had to be tackled.

Anna and The Stove did not get on. From its habit of smoking furiously and slowly dying whilst under her care, Anna had concluded that it did not like her. Sasha and The Stove got on like a—well, like a house on fire. Obviously.

Eyeing The Stove in the manner of one approaching a sleeping snake, she opened the door of its firebox. Sasha had offered to lay the fire for her before leaving for the hills that morning, but she had dismissed the offer with casual ease. In the cold light of reality, she was beginning to think it had been arrogance.

She carefully began to stack wood, kindling and paper in complex layers. This done, she struck a match and held it to the pyre, praying it would take. The fire did take, but only after a ridiculous amount of blowing, poking and tinder-adding had been done in its honour. Smarting at The Stove's rudeness, Anna slammed its firebox door shut and jerked the handle closed.

While The Stove heated the kettle sitting on its hotplate with resentfully smouldering reluctance, Anna began picking over and washing the blackberries.

By the time she had finished this task and prepared the dry ingredients for the bread, the kettle still had not boiled. Filled with impatience, she gave The Stove's side a smack. Pain coursed through her hand as The Stove proved it had finally got its house in order. Letting out a yelp, she aimed a furious kick at The Stove.

A moment later, she was gasping and hopping whilst clutching her smarting foot in her hands.

Casting a black look at The Stove, she poured the water of the now-boiling kettle out and began to mix and knead the bread dough. The hopeful cook treated Mrs Beeton's words as though they had been uttered by the Lord God almighty and set in stone, and diverging from them would result in the dissenter being struck down by divine wrath. No measurement or instruction went un-followed.

After placing the bread dough in a tin and sitting it on the warm ledge above The Stove to rise, Anna tipped the blackberries into a big pot and put it on the hotplate. But the pot would not come to the boil. Because The Stove had almost gone out.

Muttering and cursing furiously to herself, Anna flung the firebox door open. After dodging the towering plume of smoke that burst forth, she got hold of every bit of tinder in the vicinity and stuffed it into the firebox.

This created a reasonable heat, but after waiting and watching and worrying for nearly an hour, the blackberries were showing no signs of the thickening that Mrs Beeton promised.

When a further wait resulted in no improvement, the cook decided that it must not be boiling hard enough. So she flung open the much-abused firebox door once again. Then she fed the flames, poked the coals, and puffed and blew until she was dizzy and red-faced with both heat and blowing. Even when the flames had been forced into a bright blaze, the angrily determined Anna continued to fan the flames. By the time she finished with the fire, it obediently roared up the chimney like a miniature volcano.

Mopping her sweating face, which by now felt as hot as the stovetop, Anna stood back and observed her furiously boiling cauldron of blackberry jam with great satisfaction. That should teach it not to be so damn uncooperative. Cursed thing.

'Oh, my bread!' she screamed suddenly, as her eyes chanced upon the tin.

The dough had risen so fast in the heat sent forth by The Stove that it now poured down the sides of the tin like a river of molten lava.

Armed with a big spoon, the cook dashed to rescue it. After returning the slowly fleeing dough to its tin, she thrust it into the furnace of white-hotness that was the oven.

With this mission completed, the weary cook took a well-earned moment of respite from this hell's kitchen and sunk down on the backdoor step. Hot as the noonday sun outside was, it did not match the heat inside. Holding a mug of water, she let out a sigh and relished the cooler air.

But not for long. She could still hear the roar of the fire. This was not normal. It sounded much too loud. And why was there so much smoke sitting on the still, hot air outside?

Jumping up, she ran out onto the grass. Smoke, sparks and flames spewed from the chimney. It was on fire.

Letting out a scream of terror, Anna dashed for the old wooden ladder leaning against the wall. After hastily putting the ladder against the stone chimneystack, she ran to get the pails inside, then ran down to the river to fill them.

Splashing water all down her skirt, she hauled the brimming pails back and, breathing hard, lugged them up the ladder. Choking and with tears running from her smarting eyes, she braved the billowing smoke and poured them down the chimney one after the other. After letting the empty pails fall back to the ground, Anna descended the ladder and stood back to decide on the effectiveness of the dousing.

On the evidence of the white steam now arising from the chimney, she judged the fire out. Wiping the tears from her sooty, grime-streaked cheeks, she wearily trudged for the door.

When she opened it, a cloud of Pandora's Box-like proportions burst out in her face. Coughing at this fresh assault of acrid smoke, she suddenly remembered.

'Oh, my bread!' she screamed, covering her nose with her apron and dashing to The Stove.

Upon flinging the oven door open, she beheld the smoking black cinder that was once her bread. With a groan of woe, she let the tea towel fall from her hands and pushed her dishevelled hair back from her face.

A breath of air wafted in through the open door, thinning the steam and smoke engulfing The Stove. The hotplate was covered in the blackberry jam, which had boiled over. The seared-on, caramelised jam had flowed down the side of The Stove and onto the floorboards.

She reached out a drooping hand and wobbled the pot experimentally. The jam still was not set. And the fire had been extinguished.

Letting out a moan of utter defeat, she sunk to the kitchen floor. There she sat in a heap of sooty, wet, floury, blackberry-stained misery and quietly simmering rage. With her dishevelled head hanging forlornly, she silently mourned her incinerated bread and incinerated hopes of culinary success. It was all The Stove's fault. All. If it had been less bloody-minded and impossible, none of this would have happened.

With quiet fury, she shunned the offender by turning her back on it.

She sat like this for a good half hour. Then she heard the sound of Sasha's singing approaching. When he neared the open door, the song proved itself to be *Troika Speeds, Troika Gallops*, a cheerful, jaunty song about the driver of a troika, or three-horse carriage, galloping towards his home village, where his sweetheart lives. There he halts, and his fair beloved runs out and showers him with kisses. What a song to be singing. How dare Sasha. When his booted footsteps sounded on the floorboards, she did not look up.

He knelt before her and placed a kiss on her forehead. 'Hello, little darling.'

She replied with only a sullen scowl.

'Did your jam refuse to set and boil over?' he asked kindly, still kneeling before her.

'What does it look like!'

'Perhaps the fruit was not tart enough. Did you try adding a little lemon juice?'

In this God-forsaken dustbowl at the ends of the earth, no lemons were to be had. As it went without saying that no plant as illustrious as a lemon tree would call such a place home, Anna saw no reason to speak this fact aloud.

Wearing a tight-lipped, unspeakably insulted expression, she arose with a jerk and took hold of the pot of jam. This she carried to the door in silent, murderous fury and threw outside, pot and all. This task done, the injured party sat back down on the floor and sullenly crossed her arms.

She felt his hands on her shoulders. 'Do not trouble yourself like this, little darling. Such things happen to every cook from time to time.'

In too much of a mood to even answer such nonsense, Anna merely tightened her lips further and turned her downcast head away. He did not appreciate the scale of this calamity. If he did, he would not be treating her like this.

When she heard a softly amused laugh, she almost gasped. How dare he.

His hand moved to her cheek. 'Anya, little darling, why do you not go and sit down in parlour? It will be lot more comfortable than sitting on floor.'

She resisted the hand that would tilt her chin up. 'Go away.'

Sasha wordlessly took her in his arms, got to his feet and carried her over to the kitchen table. There he sat her down on it and closed an arm around her waist. With the other hand, he cupped her cheek. 'Look at me, *doosha maya.*'

Biting her lip reluctantly, she lifted solemn eyes to meet the brown gaze seeking them.

'What troubles you?'

Anna suddenly burst into tears. 'I am so h-hopeless, so useless,' she sobbed. 'I could n-not be a good daughter, and n-now I am a b-bad wife!'

Sasha held her face between his gentle hands. 'Anya, you are good wife, good friend, good lover. I am so happy I married you. I love you and always will.'

Letting the tears roll down her cheeks unimpeded by shame, she smiled, and the tears became tears of joy, of love, of relief. She placed her hand over the one caressing her cheek. 'Sasha, my dearest husband, there is something I wish to say to you.'

'What is it, my sweet one?'

She looked shyly up at him. 'I love Russian food,' she murmured with maidenly modestly. 'Especially kasha. It is the best dish ever invented.'

'Oh Anya!' he laughed, embracing her tightly. 'You really had me—I thought you were about to tell me some tender secret!'

She laughed too and hugged him close. 'That *was* a tender secret!'

Soon, the defeated little cook was deeply engaged with making a meal of her husband instead. To the accompaniment of breathy sighs and coquettish giggles, Mrs Beeton slid closer and closer to the table edge. As the temperature in the kitchen rose once more, Mrs Beeton was pushed right to the brink by the aspiring cook's head as it touched down on the tabletop.

When the cook's husband touched down on his wife a moment later, Mrs Beeton was sent plunging off the precipice. But the clatter of Mrs Beeton hitting the floorboards went unnoticed. The man of the house's murmured words of love and failed cook's giggles and gasps of pleasure almost entirely drowned it out.

Meanwhile, covered in burnt, sticky jam, black soot and flour, The Stove sat sulking resentfully as the humble Table outdid it in an astonishing upset. Seeing The Table usurp it in the 'bringing to the boil' stakes with such white-hot success crushed The Stove's pride. It was never the same again.

The Table, however, was conceited in its triumph. Merely to be a stage upon which the drama happened was a poor thing. It needed to be the *centre* of attention. Luckily for it, there was one folio remaining on its top, and the fact of one of its legs being a little shorter than the others (which hitherto had been a cause of great and lasting shame to it) provided the perfect means. The low corner dipped, and with it slid the thick folio.

Closer and closer to the edge of the precipice it came. Then Anna, in tossing aside the shirt she had just pulled off her husband's body, brushed the teetering folder with her arm. This was the final straw that sent it plunging over the brink.

During its flight the folder fell open, and all the sheets of paper contained within burst into the air like a flock of startled white birds. They floated like feathers on the warm air, drifting to every corner of the tiny room before falling to earth.

At the sound of them alighting, Anna let out a gasp and a cry. Pushing Sasha off, she struggled free and dashed after them. On her hands and knees she scooped them up.

But fast as she worked, new leaves kept falling from above or arriving from across the room on the breath of the breeze coming in through the open door.

Ivanovsky plucked one from the air and held it up. 'Oh Anya, they are beautiful!'

'No, they're mere scribblings; rubbish from the idle hand of a bored housewife!' she cried, snatching at it desperately.

He held it high above her reach. 'I must differ. The way in which you have drawn me as sleeping Endymion is wonderful. This self-portrait of you as goddess Selena is quite marvellous too. Artist by day, life-model by night; and all this time I did not know it!'

'Oh Sasha, it's merely an appalling doodle—one so awful I'm heartily ashamed of it!' she gasped, jumping up to reach it. 'Give it back, do please!'

'You do yourself grave disservice, *doosha maya*,' he replied, still holding it above her reach. 'At art academy with me were many men whose drawing skills were far beneath this.'

Anna barely heard him. She jumped again, more energetically. But all of the gathered-up papers were severely jolted in the process. They slipped from her hand and cascaded back across the floor.

She gasped, then let out a groan of defeat. It was too late anyway. Sasha had seen her dreadful scrawlings now. It only remained for him to ridicule her efforts, take offence at her secret portraits of him, be morally outraged at the nudes, and chastise her severely for daring to waste time on pointless things when she should have been attending to her duties as a housewife.

Anna sunk to the floor amid her scattered sketches and hung her head.

She was surprised when her husband set down beside her a moment later and picked up another of her papers. A smile spread over his lips as he looked at it. 'What an adorable watercolour. It's Jack, young son of the miners up river, is it not?'

She nodded miserably. 'Yes. I painted him when he came over to help me pick blackberries—when *I* should have been picking them and *he* shouldn't have been eating them.'

'Truly wonderful... Oh, and this one!' he cried, catching sight of another painting. 'The river at bottom of garden. And with me as river god!' he added with a laugh. 'There am I believing you are writing letter, while all the time you are sketching me as I bathe!'

Anna could feel her cheeks burning once more, this time from the shame and humiliation blazing within her instead of from the stove's hot flames. 'I am so sorry, Sasha. I don't know why I did such a dreadful thing.'

Cringing at the mere thought of anyone respectable seeing her collection of drawings and paintings, she put a shielding foot over a drawing lying nearby. She hoped the move had appeared undeliberate, although it was doubtful. Even so, looking a little sillier was a small price to pay for no longer having *that* drawing exposed for all the room to see.

Those hot nights when Ivanovsky had flung off the sheets in despair at what he considered temperatures worthy only of the very hottest part of hell had provided Anna with a great opportunity. In the depths of the night when sleep evaded her, as it often did, she would light a small candle and by its soft golden glow trace every beloved line of her sleeping husband's form onto her snow white paper. As he slept, that gentle, angelic smile always played on his lips, and it was this smile she wished most of all to capture. Yet so far it had eluded her. The many drawings of Sasha Ivanovsky's sleeping face littering the floor could attest both to her determination to succeed and to her failure so far.

Sasha looked up from the drawing he held. 'You have done nothing that needs forgiving. They are wonderful, all of them.'

'You are not angry with me? Not—not *disgusted* with me?' she asked in a small, uncertain voice, finally daring to look at her husband.

'No! Why would I feel such a thing?'

The genuine surprise in his loving face suddenly made Anna feel ashamed for a different reason. 'I do not know,' she replied quietly, staring glumly down at her hands. 'Perhaps it is because I am a silly, small-minded creature who assumes that everyone else is likewise afflicted.'

'Anyone who says your drawings and paintings are anything less than perfectly beautiful is fool.'

She took note of the slightly raised eyebrow and subtly challenging emphasis that accompanied his final word. She knew he was right. She *was* always doubting him and questioning him. Why could she not simply accept the truth? He was a saint, a perfect angel.

'Oh Sasha, I do love you so!' she cried, throwing her arms around his neck and burying her face against his warm shoulder. 'My poor darling, always having to endure the nonsense of such a foolish wife!' she added enthusiastically, and kissed him.

Still feeling dreadfully guilty, she added a shower of kisses to that one, all delivered tenderly to the neck of her long-suffering man.

'*Solnishka*, sometimes it is just better when you are not talking...' he sighed.

'You are right, darling. You are always right,' she replied, between kisses.

'Thank you. Ahhhh...perfect—oh, did I tell you my art dealer friend Nicolai might be visiting later?'

She stopped kissing abruptly. 'No.'

'Well, now I have. Do continue with what you were doing before, my little rabbit...' he murmured dreamily.

'You wait until now to tell me this? Look at the state of this kitchen!' She accompanied this demand with a finger pointed directly at the stove and the tone of rising panic all respectable housewives adopt in this situation.

Ivanovsky had now unwillingly opened his eyes. 'Nicolai will not even notice, little honeybee,' he replied in his most soothing voice. 'Unless it is a drawing, an oil on canvas or watercolour on paper, he does not care about it at all.'

She was not entirely reassured, but decided against contesting it. If her pledge to love, honour and obey was not to sound altogether like empty words, she must try harder than she hitherto had been. 'Of course, darling. You know him better than I do.'

He smiled. 'Thank you.'

Now that this little matter had been resolved, Anna resumed where she had left off. After a lingering kiss that was passionately returned by him, she moved her lips slowly and tenderly across his cheek and arrived at the dip in his neck just below his ear. This was the place where she knew he liked to be kissed most of all.

A long sigh of pleasure greeted her caressing lips as they explored this sweetest spot. But after only a few moments, she felt his muscles move beneath her lips. 'Anya darling, I was thinking…'

She paused her kissing once more. Without even noticing it, she had tensed. 'Yes?'

'Nicolai is always looking for new artists. I feel sure he would be very interested in Mrs Ivanovsky's latest creations.'

Anna frowned. 'Mrs Ivanovsky? Which relative of yours do you mean to refer to?'

He just smiled.

'What—me?'

He nodded.

'No, Sasha! No, no, no!' she cried, spinning away from him in a panic and beginning to scoop her scattered drawings and paintings up. 'No one—hear this—no one, is ever going to see these! I don't care what you think you know, in this you are wrong! These drawings are sheer rubbish and you are never going to convince me otherwise, no matter what rot you tell me!'

Ivanovsky was obliged to get up in order to prevent his wife tearing the papers he partly set on, she was pulling so hard at them.

'And no humbug about wives obeying their husbands will sway me either!' she shouted over her shoulder as she stuffed the collected papers into a drawer.

Standing beside the table, Ivanovsky did not reply. He just smiled to himself. Only she ever said anything about wives obeying their husbands. He never had, and never would, make such a demand.

Upon looking out the door, he saw a figure striding up the dusty path leading to the cottage. The man was silhouetted against the flaming orange burnt onto the sky by the setting sun. On his broad, bear-like shoulders he carried a heavy suitcase as though it weighed no more than a feather, and he whistled the tune *Kalinka* as he went.

Ivanovsky's secret smile deepened. Nicolai was the most kind-hearted and jovial of men. Anna would not last beyond five minutes before every one of her paintings and drawings was in his hands.

Sasha Ivanovsky reached for his dusty shirt and began pulling it on. 'Anya, I see Nicolai coming up road. You might wish to button up your dress and tidy your hair a little.'

Anna was down on her hands and knees fishing under the stove for the sketches hiding just out of reach beneath it. 'What!' she screamed, leaping to her feet.

The look on her husband's face left no room for hope. The dreaded man really was moments away. Anna's hands flew first to her completely open dress, then to her wild, dough-caked hair. After a few desperate rakes with her fingers, she gave up on her hair and suddenly noticed her hands. They were filthy; the nails purple, the palms floury and the backs sooty. Frantically she wiped them on her apron. But this only added a coating of sticky jam and an extra dusting of flour.

She could have cried.

If Ivanovsky had not held out his hand to her and bestowed his most loving smile upon her, Anna would indeed have burst into tears. On bare feet (her shoes had been soaked in the rush to bring water to the fire and discarded), she stepped across the battered, flour-dusted floorboards and took the offered hand.

Ivanovsky drew Anna towards him and put his arm around her. 'See, he comes.'

Almost too spent to think, Anna leaned against her husband as a drooping, wind-tossed flower leans against the stake provided by a thoughtful gardener. She followed Sasha's gaze out of the cottage door and down the dusty path.

There, in a field of gold, stood a towering bear of a man wearing the blazing sun—that, at any rate, was how he appeared to her eyes. The golden flames haloed about him were the last rays of the burning sun sinking to earth behind him, caught in his long, wild hair, and the field of golden grasses too were gilded not by earthly gold, but by the tongues of celestial fire cast upon their straw-coloured stalks.

Anna looked back up at Sasha's face. His contemplative eyes met the future peacefully. No fear dwelt within. Then Anna looked from his serene, gentle face back to the man standing before them.

And for the first time in her life, Anna was not afraid.

The End

Historical Note

THE places that appear in this novel are real places and, with the two small exceptions noted below, appear under their real place names.

For dramatic reasons, I have given Aramoana a church. I believe that it is Pourere, a settlement a short distance up the coast, which had a church, not Aramoana. The other small adjustment is Gravemore. The real-life station is called Aramoana Station, and its homestead is located on a small hill slightly further back from the sea than where I have placed the house on Gravemore.

I have also taken a liberty with dates which I hope my readers can forgive: the homestead on Aramoana was built in 1894, not 1884 as Gravemore is. There were, however, homesteads on this coast by that date. The first of the sheep Anna so dislikes arrived there in 1849.

The church building at Pourere is still there, although it no longer is used as a church. The station at Aramoana is still there too, and is still farming sheep. But the wool clip has long since been carried by road rather than sea!

Printed in Great Britain
by Amazon